Fir

Single Books
Within the Folds of a Swan's Wing

WITHIN THE FOLDS OF A SWAN'S WING

JENNIFER WALKER

Within the Folds of a Swan's Wing
ISBN # 978-1-83943-929-2
©Copyright Jennifer Walker 2020
Cover Art by Louisa Maggio ©Copyright November 2020
Interior text design by Claire Siemaszkiewicz
Finch Books

Published in 2020 by Finch Books, United Kingdom.

Finch Books is an imprint of Totally Entwined Group Limited.

WITHIN THE FOLDS OF A SWAN'S WING

Dedication

For Ian, Everett and Kennedy for giving me
endless love and support in following my
dreams. For the students who amaze and inspire
me — thank you for giving me your stories to tell.

Chapter One

The whispers are like waves rippling through a mountain stream. They start out at the far side of the room then cascade into a waterfall of stolen glances and hushed tones. Their eyes briefly meet mine, then quickly look away as if caught in a trap. The rumor continues like a string of dominoes that has just been flicked, until it's made its way through the entire class and everyone is left looking straight at me.

Again.

For the zillionth time during my painfully wretched start to high school.

What now? I think to myself. *What could I have possibly done this time to deserve all this glorious attention?*

"Hey, Jodie, what's the target for? You trying to attract a bull with that red splotch? I heard they really like the smell of blood. You really should have remembered your diaper today, girl."

Sean Fedun. Ridiculously handsome Sean Fedun, with his side-swept surfer hair, his fresh, sun-kissed skin that always holds a golden glow, even in the depths of winter... Sean Fedun, who, on top of being handsome, smart and popular, is also the biggest jerk in the school and the bane of my existence.

Of course, it is Sean who notices things first, and he's the one who so callously starts the tidal wave that threatens to further drown me. I hear the gasps and murmurs before I see them, although it isn't until the wave of whispers reaches its crescendo at the other side of the room that I recognize exactly what they're all laughing about.

And that's when I feel it, damp and sticky between my legs. My face immediately flushes bright red as the moment of realization hits.

My.

Worst.

Nightmare.

Ever.

As if I'm not already teetering on the periphery of high school's social order, now my body has failed me in the most brutal way. And I know... Immediately I know and I'm hit with a panic and shock so intense that I lose my breath. I have no reaction, no solution. I know right here and now that this is the one thing — literally *the one thing* — that if it were to happen, would ruin me forever. I am forever ruined. No one will forget this. *Ever.* There is no coverup possible. There is no recovery. Slowly, as if time is suddenly filtered through an impossibly small hourglass, I turn my gaze downward to the red bullseye everyone is pointing at — the one quickly seeping through the crotch of my otherwise-white jeans.

In another reality, it could be Kerri Parker sitting across from me. Sweet Kerri Parker, who would quietly come over to me and whisper in my ear, "Jodie, I think you should excuse yourself and go to the bathroom." I would be able to slink out of the classroom without anyone even realizing I had been there in the first place.

Or it could be Maela Xing. She barely speaks English at all and would sit quietly with my secret for the entire year.

Or it could even be one of the robotics nerds. Most of them are so wrapped up in the games on their cell phones that the entire incident would go unnoticed completely.

But it's not. It's Sean Fedun. And like a zillion times before, Sean Fedun finds a way to ruin me.

It's the week right after spring break, and the entire ninth-grade class has just gathered in the auditorium to hear about the parts for the upcoming freshman spring musical. As usual, Miss Pennefore flits around like a sparrow, sorting out music sheets and audition papers, and is barely aware the class has even come in and settled down. Earlier in the afternoon, she had arranged the choir risers into something of a semicircle so that the stage would hold all one hundred and ninety-six of us a little more easily. Yes, almost two hundred ninth-grade witnesses to what is undoubtedly the most humiliating moment of my life.

Most of the kids are sitting and chatting in small groups, excited about the prospect of being one of the leads in this year's freshman production of *Annie*. As if I care one ounce about being in this play… In fact, I wouldn't be here at all except that it was mandatory. Yep, every single one of us is going to be given a part to try out for, even if we have no interest in the stupid play! An apparent attempt at letting every student feel like a *star*. *Yeah, great idea.* Make us all sing the chorus of *It's a Hard Knock Life* to the rest of the class, only to be humiliated and sent to the back row of the choir anyway. None of these kids even know what a 'hard knock life' means. It's clear by the way they've been belting it out in the hallway all week long, ever since we found out that *Annie* was the musical of choice this year. The fevered smiles plastered on their faces, raising their arms to the sky as they attempt to hold the final note in a fake vibrato...

I'm sorry, but if you actually *do* have a hard knock life, you don't go around singing about it in the middle of a suburban high-school auditorium. No, you'd be sitting in the gutter somewhere wondering why your life is a pile of garbage — which is sort of how I'm feeling now to tell the truth.

But, as it turns out, I'm a rule follower. So, despite my better judgment, I had silently trudged to music class today to get my assigned role, and I'd attempted to shrink into oblivion behind the frizzy shield of my hair. I'd even purposely sat down in the front row, the lowest riser, with the hope that no one would attempt a conversation with me. I shouldn't have worried, because, to be honest, no one typically even notices I'm around — except for today of all days, when we sit facing each other in a stupid semicircle of trust, and Sean Fedun happens to be the person sitting exactly opposite me.

Whoosh...thunk.

I feel it before I see it...the first one, at least. A slight tap on my left shoulder, as if someone is trying to get my attention, then it drops softly at my feet. And before I know it, there are dozens hurling past me, zooming past my face and knocking against my body. Before I recognize exactly what it is that they are throwing at me, another tampon bounces sharply against my chest, resting squarely in my lap. I survey the situation — tampons, pantyliners, maxi-pads and even a used tissue, all being thrown at me, all collecting at my feet like a pile of dead moths, attracted to the bug-zapper in my backyard.

And amid the snickers and belly laughs, I can make out Sean Fedun's cocky voice. "Jodie McGavin... Such a disgusting pig. What a waste of a life."

And I decide I'm not going to take it any longer. I can't. I fumble with my books when I try to stand up, spilling the entire contents of my science binder on the floor. As I reach down to pick everything up, I can't help but bend over with my rear end sticking out into the middle of the semicircle of laughing students, giving them an even better look at the bloodstained splotch than they'd had before. And what's even worse, some of the papers that have strewn all over have landed on the spots of blood I've unwittingly left on the carpeted riser. As I pick them up and try to stack them in order, bright red droplets of blood seep from one to the other, like my own personal seal. The burn in my face grows unimaginable, and it takes every ounce of strength in me not to let my humiliation spill over into a heap of tears. I will not let them see me cry. I will *not* give them that satisfaction.

I hastily grab the last of my belongings and bolt from the room as the class erupts into full-blown hysteria. I can just barely hear Miss Pennefore's shrill attempt at maintaining order as she tries to make out what has just transpired behind her back.

The *incident*.

I know this will remain a black splotch on my memory of high school. And as I run from the laughter and the mocking, all I can envision is the spreading red stain of me that will remain in the room long after I leave.

Chapter Two

The hallways are empty and the sound of my runners slapping the floor reverberates against the tiled walls as I rush to the bathroom.

Thwack-ticka-ticka-thwack. Thwack-ticka-ticka-thwack. I glance down and notice a maxi-pad stuck to the bottom of my left runner, a slap in the face if I ever saw one, like God is up there laughing at me. *You really are a joke, Jodie McGavin. Here's one more reminder of how much of a loser you are.* I do a double hop on my right foot so I can peel the sticky end of the maxi off my left and almost bail into a set of lockers as I do it. I'm so completely done with this whole situation that I smack the maxi-pad square onto a locker, sticking it there in the middle of the hallway, like my own personal memento.

I should at least be grateful that it's the middle of class so there aren't any other students lingering around to embarrass me even more. I rush into the first bathroom stall I see and slam the stall door closed, plopping myself on the toilet seat. All I want to do is melt into a pile of tears and erase this day from my memory. I know all too well that it won't disappear from the memories of my classmates anytime soon. I am desperate in my attempt to clean the whole mess up but soon discover the impossibilities of blotting a giant stain of blood off the crotch of a pair of white jeans with industrial-grade toilet paper. The more I rub, the more the toilet paper disintegrates, shredding its fibers into the denim and smudging the blood into a now dinner plate-sized splotch. The blood has started to dry to a rust color, adding to the disgusting state of things. There is no way I am going back to class.

As I squeeze myself back into my too-small jeans and do my best to suck in my belly so I can get the zipper done up, my gaze falls onto the mess of graffiti kids have scratched all over the bathroom door.

Mrs. Kelly is a cow.

Go Sabers Go!

Roses are red, violets are blue, you are so nasty, I see you taking a poo.

Love the life you live. Live the life you love. – Bob Marley

Love the life I live. Right. You tell it, Bob Marley. One too many joints, I think. Because, know what? I've tried the 'embrace yourself' thing for fifteen years and it's not working out so great for me. I reach into my bookbag for a Sharpie and scribble across all of it. It feels good just to unload and I find that when I'm finished and the door is covered in a black mess, I'm ready to unlock it and re-enter the world.

Except that when I step out of the bathroom stall, it's my own reflection in the mirror that greets me. The one person I can't really stand to look at right now.

It's not my puffy red eyes that bother me—or my dry, frizzy hair. It's not the smattering of pus-filled pimples that line my nose or even the muffin-top bulging from the waist of my jeans. It's not the fact that I stand at an awkward five feet ten inches or that my skin is about twelve shades darker than pretty much every other student in this hellhole of a school. It's the whole package. The entire 'Full Meal Deal' that makes up *me*.

What does Mr. Rutter always say? The whole is greater than the sum of its parts? Yeah. Not with me. The whole *is* the problem. Me. *I'm* the problem. All of me.

I reach for the Sharpie once more and scribble across the mirror until the glass is a warped mosaic of puzzle pieces, my reflection unrecognizable, even to me, as if the person in the mirror is trapped behind the glass and not following me around everywhere I go.

With a surge of determination, I hastily wrap my sweater around my waist and shuffle my way to the office to call my mom. It's the middle of the day, so either she's going to be taking Anna and Amy to their Tiny Tots dance class, or she'll be at home working. I'm not looking forward to this call. My mom doesn't do well with *bad optics* — things that may make her look bad. She likes things to be smooth sailing, and somehow, when it comes to me, I've always created a lot of waves.

As I enter the office doors, the head secretary raises her eyebrows at me momentarily as if to ask me why I'm out of class. It's obvious that she notices I've been crying, because she passes me a box of Kleenex as I approach her desk.

"Yes, dear, what can I help you with?"

"Um… I'm sick and I need to go home early. I just want to call my mom." As I say it, I feel the wobble in my voice that happens right before I burst into a pile of tears. I dig my fingernails into my thighs so that the pain will distract me from my feelings of self-pity.

"Well, I suppose you can. Is everything okay?"

"Yeah, I just... I just...don't feel very good. I think I'm going to throw up." She rushes to hand the phone to me and grabs another pile of tissues as she does. I glance to my right and see that Mr. Rutter's door is closed, and it fills me with an immense sense of relief. I definitely would not want to have a chat with Mr. Rutter right now. I'm already dreading the session I know we're going to need to have on Tuesday. The one where he's probably going to ask me to discuss my feelings about the incident that occurred in music class, where I'm probably going to have to relive this entire disaster *again* to him. As if I won't be reliving it every single day when I walk the hallways and hear Sean Fedun constantly making jabs behind my back.

The thought makes me want to vomit, so I turn my attention back to the secretary, who's still waiting for me to make the call. As I wait for my mom to pick up, all I can think of is the massive relief I'm going to feel once I hit the solace of my bedroom.

She finally answers on the fourth ring, clearly irritated at something.

"Yes, Sandra McGavin speaking."

"Um, hi, Mom. It's me, Jodie."

"Jodie, what's wrong? You should be in the middle of class right now." There's a sort of urgency in her voice.

"Yeah, Mom, I know. It's just that there has been a sort of incident." My thighs are stinging from my jabbing fingernails again, but it somehow does help me to fight back the tears.

"Well, are you okay, honey? What happened?"

"Yeah, I'm fine. I'm not hurt or anything. It's just that I got my period and I need to come home." I know it sounds lame and pathetic the moment it comes out of my mouth, but it's not like I can just come right out and say that my life has been absolutely and totally ruined and that the humiliation I experienced today is beyond anything I can describe.

"Oh well, Jodie, everybody gets their period. That's no big deal. Just clean yourself up and get back to class. This is really not a big deal."

"But, Mom, I'd really like to come home now." As I say the word *home*, my voice breaks suddenly, as if it's been suspended on a tightrope and the bar I'm holding has suddenly tipped to the side.

"Jodie, this is just not a good time. The twins are just finishing their dance class and Amy's been super-crabby today. I think she's got an earache again and I've just managed to book her into an appointment at the pediatrician. I just don't have time to come and get you right now. See if you can just work it out on your own, okay?"

Her response doesn't surprise me at all. I mean, I know my mom loves me and everything, but since Amy and Anna came into the picture, it seems like I float in and out of Mom's peripheral vision, like she just can't seem to focus on me for more than a minute.

"Okay, Mom. I'll figure it out. See you soon."

I turn to the secretary and tell her that my mom is just going to be picking me up outside the school's main door. She reluctantly signs me out and tells me to feel better soon.

Chapter Three

Stepping through the front door of the school at three o'clock is typically my favorite part of the entire day—like I've been breathing through a straw for eight hours and I'm finally allowed a deep breath of fresh air. I feel free and unencumbered, as if I've been wearing a scratchy and suffocating sweater all day long and I can finally slough it off. So, you'd think that today I'd be experiencing the relief more than ever as I run away from 'the incident' and have the rest of the day free to do whatever I please.

But as I walk down the front steps, my sweater still wrapped around my waist, the laughter of dozens of students still deep within the walls of the school causes the weight that usually lifts from my chest to remain sitting there.

I wander aimlessly around the schoolyard for a while, not really sure where I should go. I've never skipped class before so I'm feeling a little badass, to tell the truth. I told my mom I'd handle my situation and go back to class, so I can't really go home until school is out. I decide to grab a snack at the frozen yogurt place on the corner, but as I walk down the sidewalk, I feel like I'm getting judgmental stares from everyone I pass. It's like they all know I'm supposed to be in school, like they're all thinking I'm either a delinquent or a dropout. Why else would a sketchy-looking Black teenager be roaming the streets of Phoenix in the middle of the day? At least that's what I imagine they're thinking. Everyone just seems so judgy all of a sudden. I can't tell whether I'm just being totally paranoid or whether I'm actually being completely realistic. All I know is that I don't like it and I'm craving the soft comforter of my bed even more now. I'm at the point that I'm even debating going home to face Mom, which I know is a very bad idea. Maybe this whole skipping school thing is really overrated. If you can't even enjoy yourself, then what's the point?

I eventually make it to the corner strip mall that houses FroYoBro, one of my very favorite places in the entire world and possibly the best frozen yogurt store in the entire city. Even just standing outside in the parking lot brings my blood pressure down a bunch. I can feel it. I push open the heavy glass door and a rush of wonderful waffle-cone deliciousness fills my nostrils. It automatically brightens my spirits and brings me a sense of calm. I've never done drugs before, but I imagine this is what it feels like. One moment life is a massive pile of crap, then after a hit of something or other, *voilà*, wrapped in a warm, comforting blanket of bliss. At least that's what it looks like in the movies. And that's how FroYoBro makes me feel every single time I stop here after school.

I don't know why, but food has always done this for me. I'm not addicted or anything. It's not like I can't stop eating. It's just that I like it. It makes me feel happy.

It's like food is my ultimate companion. It's always there when I need it, it never judges and it always makes me feel better.

Mr. Rutter thinks my obsession with food started when the twins were born. He thinks I was *'craving attention and love from my parents'* and turned to food to fill the void instead. I don't know. That sounds pretty cheesy to me, like he's just trying to sound like a real therapist. I just feel like I deserve a treat every once in a while.

Like right now.

On a random Wednesday afternoon.

When every half-decent teenager is supposed to be at school.

Every half-decent teenager but me, who has just experienced the most horrific day of my entire fifteen-year old life.

So, when the person at the till asks, "What can I get you today?" I don't expect it to be a scruffy-haired, long-limbed, skinny teenage-boy with a *Hi, I'm Jared* nametag pinned onto his shirt.

I didn't expect to see any other teenagers today. I mean, aren't all of us supposed to be in school? My eyes meet his for a brief moment and it dawns on me that I'm having the same judgmental thoughts about *him* that I was assuming the strangers were having about *me. Why isn't he in school? It's a random Wednesday afternoon. All kids should be at school. Unless something is wrong with him. Let me see… What could be wrong with him? He's got to be either a loser or a badass. He sure doesn't look like a badass…*

Of course, I don't let any of these thoughts escape my mouth and instead just try to appear normal.

"Large double chocolate fudge with chocolate chips and gummy bears on a chocolate-dipped waffle cone."

I fish out the change from my backpack and stand at the side of the counter feeling self-conscious and awkward. I pretend to be immersed in the ingredient list on the side of the glass cooler, but in my peripheral vision, I catch the boy glance up to me a few times as he's mixing in my toppings. Maybe he thinks I'm the delinquent badass.

In a moment, he reaches over the top of the counter and hands me my cone.

"Here you go. Great day for an ice cream. It's um... super-hot today. You know, for March."

I don't know why he's talking to me. Do cashiers always do this? I'm having a hard time remembering. Or is he talking to me because it's really weird that I'm not in school? Or does he know about 'the incident' and he's somehow making fun of me behind my back?

I'm fully aware that my weird paranoid thoughts are not super-normal, but this is what tends to happen to me in social situations, contributing to my... um, lack of much of a social circle.

I'm awkward. I know I am. I stumble through conversations like a blind man in a maze, oblivious to the social graces every other teenager seems to inherit naturally. I know I'm not all that pretty, which, instead of pushing me to try harder with makeup and hair products like some of the popular girls in my class so clearly advertise, causes me to care even less about my appearance and my personal hygiene. And if I'm being totally honest, I'm not all that smart either. I would love to get all the stuck-up kids back in the end by striving for Harvard or Cambridge or something, ending up as some sort of Nobel Prize-winning scientist. But no... I'm lucky to get by with a B+ on most days, which just contributes to my absolute and utter invisibility. And this is why I almost always choose to just keep to myself and pray that I will survive another day in the hell that is high school.

Kids in high school survive this purgatory by enveloping themselves in a protective casing, a group of like-minded kids who make them feel a little more normal and a little less alone.

There are the popular social media junkies — 'the sprites' is what I call them. They gracefully stride through the school with their long legs and swishy hair, frequent glimpses of a smooth and taut waist visible each time they reach up to the high shelves of their lockers. They are all glitz and glam — dancers, cheerleaders and musical-theater enthusiasts, anything that shows the world just how lovely they are. And they know it too. They tweet, Instagram and Snapchat their way through high school as if the world needs evidence of their blissful existence.

Then there are the sports stars, 'the allstars' — in my book. They champion everything they touch, and one would have to be crazy to come between them and any win. Their egos grow bigger than their muscles and they barely know that anyone else even exists.

There are the science and robotic nerds. Nice enough guys, probably, but they never pull their faces out of a textbook or computer screen long enough to even care what's going on around them. Anyone would think this group would be the easiest to break into, but, in fact, they have more stringent clique rules than anyone else. And I don't make the cut.

The last group are the druggies. I suppose I could try hanging with them, but let's be honest, how far are they going to actually make it in life? I watch enough of those dismal Netflix documentaries to know that this is a surefire way to a dead-end existence. No, I'm better off by myself, even though that means I just have me.

I try to manage a smile and a quick "yeah," to Jared, so he knows I heard him, all the while trying to figure out where he fits in the high-school popularity puzzle. He's definitely not a jock. That's obvious by his almost concave chest and spindly biceps. Druggie? Well, his eyes look alert and he *is* holding a job. Robotics nerd? Definitely the type. Probably the best fit, although I've never seen him at our school. And it still begs the question… What is he doing out of school in the middle of the day?

I think about taking my ice cream outside to eat, but I'm enjoying the air conditioning in the store. Plus, I've still got a couple of hours to kill before I can go home, so I may as well spend them here as anywhere. I settle on a tiny booth in the corner, slide myself across the nylon seat and grab a book from my backpack. I'm on the last Chapter of the latest Stephen King novel and would love to finish it so I can grab a couple of new books from the library.

I'm just figuring out where I last left off when I catch Jared coming over to this side of the store. He has a spray bottle and a cloth and is going up and down the aisles to wipe booths. As he's about to pass me, a giant splotch of chocolate ice cream drips from my cone, runs down my hand and creates a little puddle on the table in front of me. I look in vain for a napkin, but before I can get up to get one, Jared is there, spritzing and wiping the mess for me.

"Um, thanks. I could have done that."

"Well, I'm just wiping off tables anyway. What are you reading?"

"Stephen King. I'm just about done, though." I hold the book up a little higher to make it obvious that I'm in the middle of reading and not really in the mood to talk.

"So, how come you're not in school?" I knew this was coming. The panic in me starts to rise. *Is there such a thing as an undercover teen cop?*

"I'm sick so I was allowed to go home early."

"You don't look sick. I mean, you're eating a giant ice cream. Plus, I'm pretty sure this isn't your home."

The nerve of him. *What the hell?* How would he know whether I'm sick or not? It's none of his business!

"Well, I am. And it's none of your business anyway. Besides, who are you to talk? You're not in school either. What? Did you drop out or something?"

"Actually, my mom homeschools me. I get all my studies done in the morning. You can learn a lot quicker when you're homeschooled. So, I work here part-time on the side."

Homeschooled? I knew he seemed weird, like a robotics nerd times ten. But at least it makes sense. I knew he wasn't a delinquent. Part of me wonders what it would be like to be homeschooled. Then you could bypass the terrible high-school experience entirely. That would be awesome. But there's something about homeschooled kids. I've heard they're all weird and antisocial — and I don't need more of that in my life.

"My name's Jared, by the way."

"I read that on your nametag." I know at this point I'm probably supposed to introduce myself and make more chitchat, but honestly, I feel like I've already pushed the limits of my random social interactions for the day, so I'm tapping out.

I make a big show of gathering all my belongings together as if I've got somewhere important to be. I don't want this conversation to go any further.

"Nice to meet you, Jared. Have a great day." I fling my backpack over my shoulder and stride out of the door into the unlikely warm spring afternoon, with a sticky hand and a racing heart.

Chapter Four

"Mom, tell her to give me back my pony! She keeps taking my favorite one and I'm trying to set up the pony show!"

"She's lying. I had it first. She was playing with the dolls and I had all the animals. She's always making stuff up!"

"Girls! Can you try to figure things out for just two minutes? I'm trying to get some work done today. Amy, Dr. Hopkins said you're supposed to take it easy. Figure it out with Anna or you're going to be heading upstairs for a nap!"

I've never been so happy to hear the impatient squeals and tantrums of my four-year-old twin sisters. It means I can sneak in the front door—stained pants and all—and slink upstairs unnoticed to the refuge of my room.

The first thing I do is tear off my stained white jeans, crumple them up and squish them into the very bottom of my garbage can. There's no way I'm going to try to salvage those, and to be honest, they're getting way too small anyway.

I don't know when it happened — me gaining all this weight. I look at my closet filled either with things I can no longer squeeze into or clothes that have enough elastic in the waistband that my size doesn't make a difference anyway.

I wasn't always like this. Fat, I mean. Well, fat, and unpopular — and ugly, and alone. But I guess no one ever starts out like this. There's no baby who enters the world ugly, dorky and unpopular. No, every baby is seen as beautiful — to someone at least. And I was no exception. I was actually the apple of my parents' eye. Which, come to think of it, was maybe part of the problem.

Before I came into the picture, my parents tried for years to have a child. They went from doctor to doctor to see what the problem was, but none of the doctors could explain it. They would just tell my parents that sometimes *it just wasn't God's will*. Well, I think that was what pushed my parents into action. They were determined to show God who was boss. They registered with an adoption agency and were so desperate for a child by that time that they checked off pretty much every single box.

Open to a girl or boy? *Yep.*

Open to a child of any socioeconomic status? *You bet.*

Open to any ethnicity or race? *Sure, why not?*

So, a mere six months after they had submitted their application, they were told that a beautiful newborn baby girl was available for adoption. The only caveat was that she was black.

My parents are as mainstream and liberal as you can get. White, middle-class, suburban professionals. They had everything they could have ever wanted in life, except for children to share it with. And, to their credit, I don't think they really cared who or what I was when they adopted me. As soon as they signed the papers, I was no longer a random black kid from an underprivileged family. I was simply their miracle baby.

I immediately became the doted-on only child who got all the attention, all the love I could ever imagine. Despite the perplexed looks of grocery store clerks and daycare workers, my mom and dad saw me as *their* child and couldn't understand why some people did a double take when I called them Mom or Dad.

So, I suppose, with all the doting and love came all the spoiling too. I remember my parents picking me up from daycare as a preschooler, lifting me high into the air and smooshing my face with a thousand kisses. They would tell me *that* was their favorite part of the day. That *I* was the favorite part of the day. We would go home together, and they would give in to every request I would make. An extra cupcake for dessert? Sure thing. Froot Loops for breakfast? Of course. Seven new stuffies for my already-full bed? Anything for our sweetheart.

My very favorite parts of those days, though, were the endless hours we just spent together as a family. Long family walks to the park, reading countless bedtime stories and snuggling together until I fell asleep.

Despite the fact that they had to go through a third party to get me, my parents had always seen me as their miracle child. All those years of trying had finally ended in a crescendo, which was me. And for a long time, that was good enough. *I* was good enough.

My parents never let on that they were trying to have another baby after they had adopted me. I mean, I knew my parents loved children and they truly loved being parents. But at the time, I didn't really know how babies were made so I wasn't aware of the science behind it. They always told me how precious I was to them. I believed it.

That was, until that one day in fifth grade when my mom and dad announced to me that they were pregnant, and that it was supposed to be twins.

'Jodie, you know how special you are to us, don't you?' Mom held my hands and looked me straight in the eye. *'We love you so much and are so grateful that God gave you to us.'*

They always told me how special I was to them, so I didn't really see it coming. I nodded and looked toward Dad to see some sort of glimmer of what they were going on about. Maybe they'd found my birth parents and wanted me to meet them? Maybe one of them had some sort of sickness and was heading to the hospital? I was prepared for just about anything other than the nuclear bomb that they dropped on me.

'Well, we're so excited to welcome some new and very special members into our family. We're pregnant and it looks like it's going to be twins!'

This was not on my radar. I remember not really understanding the words that came out of my mom's mouth. I remember looking down at her squishy tummy and wondering how two human beings could be in there. I remember thinking that maybe two new *real* babies would mean they didn't need or want me anymore.

Like every child on the planet, I had just assumed the family we had was the family we were always going to be. We were fine, just the three of us, and I didn't see much good in adding two babies to the mix. No one sees a three-legged stool and suddenly decides it would work better if two more legs were glued onto it—because two more legs would just make it wobbly and possibly topple over. Two more legs would mean it was no longer a stool. No, our family was perfect the way it was. At least, I always thought so. Then that little voice in the back of my head started talking to me, started filling me with the first whispers of self-doubt that now rage inside my brain all day long.

I'm not their real *child and I'm not good enough. I never really was good enough.*

It's like I had been an understudy, just filling the role while the stars of the show were waiting in the wings to jump in.

Looking back, I'm sure my parents must have used some sort of fertility treatment, because there's no way a forty-year-old randomly gets pregnant with twins after years of supposedly trying for a baby. I think that was what hurt the most. They told me I was their miracle baby. They told me I made their lives perfect. And it turns out it was all a lie. They were secretly always wanting more. I was never actually good enough for them.

My mom's pregnancy was considered 'high-risk', because of her age and because she was having twins. So, she was put on bed rest almost from the start. In terms of my mom's job, it actually worked out okay, because she works with online banking and finance and spends most of her days on the computer anyway. So, she was able to just work from home, in the comfort of her bed. But what changed the most was our time as a family. We no longer went for walks to the park after dinner. My dad ended up taking on most of the household chores since my mom was laid up, so he was often busy cooking and cleaning and, I think, just sort of forgot I was around.

That's when I started spending more time alone in my room. My bedroom turned into a sort of refuge for me — a place where I felt important and valued, even if only by my stuffed animals.

To this day, my room is my oasis, my happy place filled with all my favorite things. What I may lack in social connectedness, I make up for in little delights.

Like my four-hundred-thread-count bedspread that feels as soft as silk... I splurged and used the four hundred bucks Mom gave me for back-to-school clothes to buy that instead. She was outraged and totally floored that I would start high school with items from the clearance rack at Walmart. But I don't care about clothes. It's not like I'm going to look good in anything I wear anyway, so what's the point? My bed, though...? Well, I would spend the entire day in it if I could.

My extensive collection of Stephen King books... He's my favorite author by far, but really, I love pretty much any thriller that gets me hiding under the covers. The thing about scary books is that I completely forget who I am and what my life is all about when I read them. It's like every cell in my body is so entrenched in the scary shit of the book that there's no possible way I can even contemplate my own existence while I'm reading. For a little while, when I read Stephen King, I don't even matter. My body is just a feeling of suspense…and fear, and terror and somehow — I don't know — I love the *aliveness* of that.

Then there's my greatest accomplishment as of yet…my origami collection. Sounds super-dorky… I get it. But I don't know. Somehow I got hooked into origami a few years back, and it's like the one thing that I'm really good at. Great, actually. Maybe one of the best.

At some point right before the twins were born, when I was starting to spend more time by myself because my parents were so obsessed with their *What to Expect When You're Expecting* phase, I picked up a book about origami at the library. I was ten or eleven at the time, and up until then I usually stuck to fantasy novels or the occasional anime book. But something about the cover of this one book captured my attention. On it was a single white origami swan, flawless in its shape and folds. I wanted to learn to make something so beautiful, so perfect. So, I brought the book home and attempted my creation.

At first origami was difficult for me. I lacked attention to detail, and I seemed to get the folds all wrong. I crumpled paper after paper in an attempt to replicate the beautiful creation on the cover. To me, time stopped while I was folding that paper. I needed all my focus and concentration on the task at hand, and I forgot, just for a little while, about how my life was soon going to change as these new babies were about to come into the world, and how my life had already changed, even though they had yet to arrive.

But before I knew it, I was pressing the last corner of my swan together and I held my masterpiece up in front of my face. It gave me such a feeling of success and satisfaction that I'd created this magic all by myself, that I was good enough to make something so beautiful. I remember cupping the paper bird delicately in my palms, feeling like it was my baby, like it was mine. I actually cried. I bawled like a baby and my heart felt like it was going to burst out of my chest with pride. Pride for folding a stupid piece of paper? *Yep.* Pathetic, I know. But you know what? I cleared off an entire bookshelf for that piece of origami and placed it up there as if it were the biggest trophy I had ever won. It still sits up there today—almost as if I finally found myself in the folds of that swan's wing.

Chapter Five

I take a huge, deep breath, close my eyes, then count to five. Opening the door to the school auditorium feels like the equivalence of bungee-jumping off the Grand Canyon. It's been three days since 'the incident' and school has been horrendous — even more horrendous than usual, that is.

Yesterday, my first day back after it happened, I was welcomed to school with a smattering of maxi-pads stuck onto the door of my locker. Luckily most of the students were too cheap to continue that little charade for much longer, so my locker was clear when I showed up to school today. I thought I could finally put things behind me, that I could just turn invisible once more. But this morning during language arts class, Ms. Kelly started going on about the importance of using proper punctuation in our writing. I was just busy doing my thing and trying to fade into oblivion when Sean Fedun blurted out, "Why don't you ask Jodie McGavin? She's the expert on periods." Everyone started howling as I slunk down lower in my chair.

The worst part of it was that Ms. Kelly didn't have any idea what he was talking about, and gratefully asked me to point out all the specific uses of punctuation in a passage she was showing us. *Come on, really?* Isn't every teacher supposed to take some sort of class on empathy or 'with-it-ness' — something that would give her some sort of clue as to what was going on? And, of course, I had to go along with it and finish her little exercise. It's not like I can excuse myself to go to the bathroom anymore…

But my one point of relief so far has been that I've at least been able to escape music class. Well, until now, that is. My mom called in to the school and explained that I have a phobia of public speaking and public displays of performance, thank the Lord. I convinced her that was why I was so upset the other day, and she bought it hook, line and sinker.

So, I got to avoid having to do actual auditions, and Miss Pennefore settled on simply giving me a part in the chorus — which is fine, I guess. I can hide myself in the back row and maybe no one will even notice if I don't show up on production night.

But I do have to be there for choir rehearsal, which means I have to enter the auditorium for the first time since 'the incident'…right…now.

I have literally been having nightmares about this exact moment — about pulling open the heavy auditorium doors and having two hundred obnoxious teenagers pointing and laughing at me as I walk in.

So, I brace myself for the worst as I wrench open the door.

But nothing happens.

There are a few kids gathered around the piano, a bunch more going over their music sheets on the risers and, as I stand here dead in my tracks in the doorway, three more students bustle past me as if I'm not even there.

As if I'm not even there.

Words that used to torture me and scar me, but words that I now welcome warmly with open arms. I crave the anonymity that I previously secured, the safety that 'being a no-one' affords me. And it's hard for me to believe, but I almost feel hopeful in this moment that there is a chance I can maybe melt into oblivion once more.

I keep my head bowed and shuffle my way straight to the far side of the room, to the very back riser. I don't dare sit down. That would be tempting fate to replay itself all over again. But instead, I just stand in the shadowy spot out of reach of any of the stage lights.

A few moments later the risers fill, the lead characters take their places at the front of the stage and Miss Pennefore claps to get everyone's attention.

"Hello, everyone, and welcome. I know we're all very excited to be joining together today to begin working on the chorus songs for the play. And we're grateful that you have all chosen to take the part that was assigned to you. We here at Maple Ridge believe that all parts are star parts, and that those of you in the risers are just as important as those with lead roles."

A few kids roll their eyes and laugh at that last line, and it brings me a surprising feeling of connection with the rest of the chorus. After all, we're all in this together, aren't we?

One of the student stage helpers begins to hand out the booklets full of the songs we're going to have to memorize and sing. I take one without looking up and turn to a random page, knowing full well that my mouth will not be opening once during the entire production.

Forty-five minutes left. *Only forty-five minutes…*

The pianist begins playing the opening notes to *It's a Hard Knock Life* and the entire chorus joins in right on key. Well, everyone except for me. To be honest, they all sound pretty good and I find myself sort of lost in the moment, enjoying just listening to the music…until Miss Pennefore abruptly stops mid-phrase.

"Wait, wait, wait. I'm sorry, my friends, but to have a chorus, I need *all* my chorus members singing, and I need your eyes up on me so you can see the cues. You, in the back, with the baggy T-shirt…"

It takes me a moment to realize she's talking to me, as I thought I was so well-hidden in the shadows. I swallow hard then answer her.

"Um, me? Yeah…?

"Yes, dear. You need to sing to be in a chorus. And in order to know what to sing, you need to have your eyes focused on me, your director. But with your hair totally covering your face like that, well, how are you supposed to see anything? You should know by now that your hair ought to be tied up in choir rehearsal so it's not distracting for you or the audience. Go ahead. Tie it back so it's off your face."

I still haven't gotten over the fact that she is speaking directly to me, and I'm cursing myself for having the nerve to show up here today. What was I thinking?

But the bigger problem is that I don't have an elastic on me and so I have no way of pulling back my hair.

You see, my hair has always been sort of a security blanket for me, a protective shield that I could hide behind, a way for me to brave the world. If I couldn't see them, they surely couldn't see me. And I like that this frizzy wall covers me up, shuts me out and pulls me away from the world. And now she wants to take it away?

Before my mom's pregnancy with the twins, my hair was a badge of honor for my mom. Being as white as Wonder Bread, my mom had no clue what to do with my crazy African-American hair. When I was a baby, it was somewhat easy. She would leave it natural in a cute baby 'fro and simply stick in a little bow or headband to announce that I was a girl. But as I became school-age, she decided we needed to enlist the help of professionals. I give my mom a lot of credit. She researched hair salons all over the city that specialize in doing little girls' braids and cornrows. I'm sure she felt self-conscious waltzing into a Black hair salon as a white mom, but she didn't even flinch. She asked for the top stylist and sat there beside me for three hours while I had my hair twisted into tight little braids. She was so pleased with the results—and the gushing comments of strangers—that she made a point of bringing me into the salon every three or four weeks for a new style. It was almost like figuring out how to manage my unruly locks gave her legitimacy over having an African-American child. Every three weeks she was able to give herself a gold star for parenting.

But once she became pregnant, the trips to the salon ended abruptly. My dad was capable of doing a lot of things, but managing his daughter's unruly hair was not in the mix. Looking back, I suppose my mom should have figured something out. I mean, we could have had someone come to the house or she could have gotten a friend to take me. But honestly, when she was growing two tiny human beings inside her, scheduling my hair appointments just wasn't a priority.

So, starting in fifth grade, when my mom was still in her first trimester, I just let my hair start growing out. At first, it got all super-frizzy at the roots where the braids had grown. Eventually it got so bad that even my dad noticed and agreed that we needed to do something about it. With his desire for efficiency, he took me straight to some cheap salon in the mall and asked the hairdresser there to just cut off the braids. I couldn't believe what I saw in the mirror when the hairdresser turned me around. It was like I had a scraggly lion's mane framing my face, made worse by the fact that the hairdresser clipped on two little bows that acted as ears.

I went home and spent the rest of the afternoon attempting to smooth out my mop of frizz with a bunch of different types of oils. All that actually did was make my hair stick straight out instead of straight up. The funny thing was that Mom didn't even seem to notice or care. Looking back, I think that's when I first felt forgotten, like I didn't really matter anymore. A year prior to that, my mom would have torn a strip off my dad then marched me back to the salon to have the whole situation resolved. But no… She simply stroked my hair, kissed the top of my head and reassured me that it would soon grow out.

And it did. By the time the twins arrived a few months later, my hair had grown long enough that it hung almost to my chin. It still poked out at funny angles, but the curls had relaxed slightly so if I slathered it in oil and tucked it behind my ears, I looked presentable enough.

And this is how things still are today. My hair is kind of a new badge of honor for me. It's grown to resemble a bush of dried-out tumbleweed and acts like a wall I can hide behind anytime I don't want to interact with the world.

Which would be right now…in choir rehearsal, as two hundred students have all turned to look at me and somehow the stage lights have pivoted just enough for me to be centered right in the middle of the brightest spotlight.

"Um, I don't have an elastic…so—"

"Sorry. Speak up. I can't hear you. What are you going on about?"

"I have no…um—"

"Here, Jodie. Just take it." I feel a nudge on my right side and look down to see a plain black elastic sitting loosely in an outstretched palm.

Rebecca Sherman, one of the loveliest and kindest of the sprites, best friend to the iconic Kayla Sutton— Queen Bee Sprite if you ever saw one—and I've never been able to figure out that friendship. Rebecca has always had an empathy about her that Kayla lacks Like she is at the top of the popularity food chain because that's what is expected of her, not necessarily because that's what she wants.

She quickly elbows me again, raising her eyebrows as if to say, *'what are you waiting for?'* And, with just a moment of hesitation, I grab the elastic and awkwardly try to tame my mane into somewhat of a ponytail behind my head. It is a simple gesture, one that most people would never think twice about. But for me, it is everything.

This small kindness means that Miss Pennefore is off my case and back to hitting the high notes of *Tomorrow*.

It means the two hundred other students in the room have already swiveled their heads back to the front of the auditorium. And it means, for a short while, that Jodie McGavin doesn't have to be the joke of the day.

I don't know if people like Rebecca Sherman realize that something so small can mean so much. That one small gesture can change someone's world. In that moment, it did mine.

Chapter Six

Tuesday has somehow come around again and I sit here waiting for Mr. Rutter on one of the scratchy plastic chairs outside his office. Mr. Rutter is the school psychologist, and since the beginning of the year, he has taken me on as one of his — I don't know — patients, I guess.

When I arrived in September, I was reluctant to make friends. It's not that I didn't want to. It's just that I don't seem to click with anyone here. It doesn't bother me much, to tell the truth. I've come to like the silence and solitude that loneliness affords me — more time for books, for origami, for daydreaming of when I'm all grown up and I don't have to be at this stupid school anymore.

But the school administration seems to be more concerned than anyone else about my lack of social connectedness and has set me up to talk to Mr. Rutter once a week. I actually don't mind talking to him every week, as it gives me an excuse to get out of class for an hour. Every Tuesday morning I wait with anticipation during math class, the tick of the clock getting louder and louder until it strikes ten-fifteen, when I silently pack up all of my belongings and escape to the relative safety of Mr. Rutter's office.

Mr. Rutter is a dwarf of a man, just barely making it over five feet. It's almost to the point that I keep thinking maybe something's wrong with him. Maybe he didn't produce enough growth hormone when he was a teenager and it stunted him to this height. Or maybe he just has tiny parents and bad genetics. Whatever the reason, I tower over Mr. Rutter, which I quite like. It gives me a sense of power, a feeling that I can steer our little meetings in whichever direction I choose, because really, what can he do about it?

I often wonder if Mr. Rutter got bullied as a child. That would explain why he chooses to sit and chat with awkward teenagers like me for a living. Maybe he feels some sort of redemption when he helps us navigate our twisted paths of adolescence? It's like he's giving himself a second chance as well. For me, choosing to be a guidance counselor in a high school would be like living in an eternal hell. It would be like reliving the worst days of my life over and over again. No, I can't wait to leave this place and I will never look back.

But, like I said, I don't mind talking to Mr. Rutter. It doesn't really feel like counseling or therapy or whatever. He doesn't insist on me talking about my feelings or role-playing social situations — well, at least not all the time. We just talk and joke, both of us happy to find a one-hour reprieve in the middle of the week.

But I don't even know how I'd start talking about 'the incident' with him. I'm pretty sure he wouldn't be all that comfortable talking about it either. I don't know a single middle-aged man who willingly discusses periods with a fifteen-year-old girl. I mean, my dad's not even comfortable picking up maxi-pads for me and my mom at the grocery store.

I've been dreading Tuesday morning all weekend because, of course, I know 'the incident' will be brought up. As much as I appreciate how he tries to help me, sometimes I just wish Mr. Rutter would let me be. I'm better dealing with things the same way I always do. I stay quiet, I keep my head down, and I just count the minutes until the school day is done. I sometimes wonder about fighting back, putting Sean Fedun and his little posse in their place. But what is there to say? What could I possibly do that would dent Sean's armor even the tiniest bit? It's easier for me to just do my best to ignore them and one day it will all go away. It has to.

Last week in our session, Mr. Rutter told me we were going to be working on *establishing a positive self-esteem* — his words, not mine — and my assignment was to come up with at least ten things that I'm exceptional at. 'Exceptional' was his word too. I mean, how many people are really *exceptional* at anything? Does eating half a cheesecake in one sitting count? Or how about fading into the same exact color of pea-green soup as the walls of the school's hallway, so that no one even notices that you're there?

I didn't think he would appreciate my humor, so I took the assignment home and wrote a list from one to ten. At number one I wrote 'origami'. Numbers two through ten just remained empty for the week. I mean, after 'the incident' and all the humiliation that followed, I haven't really felt exceptional at anything other than being exceptionally humiliated.

So, in order to avoid having Mr. Rutter look down at my paper with disappointment and begin discussing the meaning of all that empty space, I brought in my most recent origami creation today as a distraction. Usually my passion for origami is a private thing and I don't typically show anyone my collection. But Mr. Rutter is the one exception, as he seems to be quite impressed by what I make. I've gotten really good over the past few years and I have all of my pieces organized neatly in my room.

On one shelf are all of my birds, together with the special swan I made. But joining it are dozens of different avian versions — from the pale and streamlined doves and cranes to the brightly colored paper parrots and blue jays. You wouldn't think there would be all that much difference between an origami robin or a hummingbird, but it's surprising how one corner folded this way or that can make the bird appear to be perched on a ledge or in full flight.

I have a shelf of insects, like grasshoppers and dragonflies. My mom hates this shelf, as she thinks they look so real. I once made the mistake of attempting a cockroach in the kitchen. My mom came home from work to find the kitchen floor littered with a thousand paper roaches. She screamed at the sight of them, momentarily thinking they were real, then lost her mind when she realized she had been deceived. She scooped the entire lot into a big black garbage bag and put it out into the garage. I decided to do my origami in my room from then on.

Another shelf is full of large land animals like cheetahs and lions. That's where I keep my elephant sculpture. Next to the swan, it's got to be my favorite creation. The elephant reminds me who I am, even if that isn't the greatest thing to be reminded of. I remember the day I made it.

The memory of it has a way of flickering on and off in my brain, like a neon vacancy sign at a sleazy motel. With each flash comes a feeling of panic and shame that I try to push down deeper inside.

Fifth grade — right around the time the twins were born and mom and dad were practically living at the hospital. We were studying the Indigenous Cultures of North America. Our teacher had us doing a writing project that involved us discovering who our spirit animals were then writing a paragraph about why the animal we chose represented us so well. We got to do this little online quiz that asked us questions like —

On a perfect day, would you choose to —
A. Play at the park
B. Read a book alone
C. Go to a hockey game
D. Take a walk in the forest

Apparently, the questions were supposed to bring out key aspects of our personalities then, at the end, an animal match was made. Just about every kid lied and cheated their way through the quiz, as all of the girls wanted their spirit animal to be a butterfly or a peacock. And, of course, all of the boys wanted it to be a lion, tiger or some other fierce predator.

I actually did my quiz honestly. I was really curious as to what animal I would be matched with. I thought maybe a bear, with my strong and independent nature. Or maybe an eagle — wise and free. I wished wholeheartedly that a butterfly would turn up at the end, a testament that I belonged in the clique of pretty girls that had just started to form at the back of the classroom.

But an eagle, a bear or a butterfly were not what appeared on my screen when I hit submit. No. What appeared on my screen? An elephant.

In all honesty, the characteristics of an elephant really did match me perfectly. I read on to discover that an elephant is known for its serenity and strength, along with its ability to withstand adversity despite all odds. Surprisingly, elephants are known for their human-like ability to show empathy. When an individual in a herd is in discomfort, other members of the herd have been seen to make noises in communication with the hurt individual and, in some instances, elephants have been seen using touch to comfort others in the herd. An elephant covets the connection found within a family bond. Elephants appear to be independent, self-reliant beasts but actually crave the community and affection of family above everything else.

So, as I read on, thinking that maybe an elephant wasn't the worst spirit animal to be matched with, I heard a loud snicker behind me.

I turned in my chair to see Sean Fedun peering over my shoulder, reading my computer screen. Before I knew it, he was stomping around with his arm held in front of his face like a trunk. The rest of the class had no choice but to stop what they were doing and turn their attention to him.

"Check it out. There's finally proof that Jodie McGavin is a big, fat elephant after all!" He took a few more large stomps then picked up a snack bag of crackers with his outstretched arm. "Look! I'm Jodie, trying to eat everything in my path!" That's when he let out an exuberant trumpeting sound, as if to really make his point. The class joined in a chorus of chuckles and fat jokes, alternating between pointing at me and whispering quietly among themselves.

That was the first time I was truly shamed in public, the first time I was neglected as a person and seen simply as the butt of a joke. If I were stronger, or smarter or wittier, I would have had a great comeback and maybe the next four years of hell thereafter wouldn't have occurred. But instead, I sat there motionless and took it, like a heavy punching bag that lacked the will to fight back.

I went back home that day feeling worthless and empty. All I wanted to do was cry in my mother's arms and have her stroke my hair and tell me how much she loved me. But when I walked through the front door, I remembered that my mother was at the hospital, immersed in the demands of her two new daughters. Instead, my Granny Deans was there looking after me, in from Scotland for two weeks to help. She's my dad's mom, but I don't know her all that well since she has always lived so far away. I suppose she did a decent job caring for me in the strictest sense of the word, but she was brought up in a different world than I was, and her thoughts of parenting differed vastly from my parents'. She was a bit of a battleax in terms of respect and tradition, a soldier in starched linen slacks, white hair set in tight curls and a Scottish lilt to her voice. She was big on manners, housework, healthy food and keeping oneself tidy in appearance. She believed little girls should be wearing knee-high socks and smart skirts, and during that two-week vacation, she purchased an entire wardrobe for me to wear to school.

Well, the day Sean Fedun bullied me about the elephant thing, I burst through the front door after school, ready to explode into tears. Granny was in the next room, folding laundry. I caught a glimpse of myself in the mirror in the front hall—bushy hair, soft belly, fat ass and the beginnings of two small mounds on my chest, all tucked into the wrappings of a navy-blue sweatshirt and gray leggings two sizes too small. It was definitely not a 'Granny-approved' outfit.

"Hello, Jodie. How was school today?" she called from the other room. Granny then walked through the front hall and stopped abruptly in her tracks. "I hope you didn't actually wear that outfit today. It looks like you came out of the garbage bin. And what happened to your hair, dear? Remember how we talked about pulling it up off of your face and maybe using some clips or a headband. You really need to start taking better care of yourself. You have such a beautiful smile. It's just that..." Granny's voice droned off, my psyche unable to handle any further criticism for the day. I realized right then that Granny hadn't even looked at me. She didn't see *me* at all. I really was invisible and insignificant. I grabbed a bag of chips and trudged upstairs to my room, knowing that by stuffing my face I could temporarily fill that void inside me.

I sat for several hours that night folding and refolding dozens of pieces of paper until my garbage bin was overflowing and paper cuts were stinging my fingers. Before I went to sleep, I gently placed the folded edges of a sleek gray elephant beside my swan with an exhausted sense of resignation.

Esme. Esme the elephant. That was what I was going to call her. And she was going to remind me to stand strong against the jerks of the world like Sean Fedun. I didn't need him. I could shut him out. In fact, I could shut everyone out.

When I gave the elephant the name Esme, I simply thought it sounded exotic and elegant. Perhaps I had just read the name in some book and it stuck to me? But a few weeks later, I decided to look up the meaning as I really didn't know the origin. And do you know what I found Esme to mean? *The beloved.* Yes, Esme is my beloved. For a long time, it made me so sad to see her sitting on that shelf all by herself. So, a few months ago, I spent one entire afternoon creating a whole slew of elephants to put together, to give Esme a family. I intricately attached each elephant to another by folding one's trunk into another's tail until they formed a perfect circle. Now Esme was never alone, never unprotected, despite having to share that shelf with lions and hyenas.

So here I am now, a fifteen-year-old self-described loner, with the same origami obsession I had at age eleven. I look down at my lap as I sit awkwardly by myself in the office, and I'm suddenly embarrassed that I brought along my newest creation. It seems juvenile and pathetic. I mean, it is beautiful—an exquisite butterfly that flaps its tissue-paper wings when you squeeze its tiny legs just so. The steps involved were super-intricate and it was made with crepe paper, far more delicate than what I usually work with. I don't know whether Mr. Rutter will be impressed. *Maybe.* I'm just hoping he'll be impressed enough to forget talking about the self-esteem list or the fallout from 'the incident', which are probably in the forefront of his mind.

While I'm lost in thought, I hear the bell above the main office door tinkle, as an indication that someone has just walked in. A girl with a long ponytail of mousy-brown hair and a pale face free of makeup walks in arm-in-arm with a woman who I suppose is her mom. It strikes me as a bit weird for a couple of reasons. First, I'm pretty sure I'm the only ninth-grade student in the entire school who doesn't wear makeup. There is no way one of the sprites would show up without their face looking like it was the canvas in an art-deco gallery. Second, what high-school student on *Earth* walks around holding arms with her mom? Even I know that is social suicide.

I'm curious to find out more about this new girl but don't want to overtly stare or eavesdrop. I know only too well how it feels to be scrutinized by others. So, I stay intent on looking down at the paper butterfly sitting on my lap, willing Mr. Rutter to open his door so I can simply exit the scene.

I feel a body brush past me then plop down into the chair right next to mine. Out of the corner of my eye, I see that it's the girl who has just walked in, and I see her mother chatting with the secretaries at their desk across the room. I wonder why she chooses to sit in that seat, as the office is lined with a dozen chairs, every other one of them empty. I hope she isn't one of those people who starts up conversations with random strangers, asking personal questions that are really inappropriate in a stranger-stranger relationship.

Instead of looking up and acknowledging her, I keep my kinky curtain of hair shielding my face and try my best not to draw any attention to myself.

But suddenly, I hear a soft *tap-tap-tap* sound and see a rocking movement in my peripheral vision. The legs of the chair the girl sits on must be uneven on the tile floor. She begins rhythmically rocking back and forth and the chair legs make soft knocking at each succession. I think it's just a momentary thing at first, like maybe it's something this girl does when she first sits down and is nervous. But after several minutes of this persistent rocking, I start to get really annoyed. After all, until she came, I was enjoying a moment of peace and quiet. Not only that, but each time she rocks, her leg brushes against mine in an unnaturally intimate gesture for two teenagers not having ever met before.

So finally, I turn to her and say, "Excuse me, but would you mind stopping that? You keep bumping me."

Most other kids my age would either rush to apologize or would respond with a snide comment and a roll of their eyes. She does neither. Instead, she mimics my tone perfectly, repeating back, "You keep bugging me. You keep bugging me." All the while, she just keeps rocking without missing a beat.

I'm not sure if something is wrong with her or whether she really is just that rude. Maybe she got kicked out of another school and is trying to get let into ours? *Oh great*, I think. *One more person to constantly taunt me.*

Except that this girl doesn't look the same as the other kids at our school. She has a glazed look over her eyes, as though she's lost in space. And she just seems to be immersed in her own world.

As I contemplate all this, Mr. Rutter appears out of his office and strides over to us.

"Well, hello, ladies. Jodie, I see you've met our new student, Bethany. Bethany, the girl you are sitting beside is named Jodie McGavin."

"Jodie McGavin, J-o-d-i-e-M-c-G-a-v-i-n, Jodie McGavin. Spelled backwards is n-i-v-a-G-c-M-e-i-d-o-J."

Huh? Is all I have time to think. *What is going on here?*

Mr. Rutter chuckles a bit then starts to clarify things.

"Bethany is visually impaired, Jodie, and she also has ASD — autism spectrum disorder. So sometimes she has a difficult time relating to others in a similar way as you or I might, and her communication with others is often different. For instance, she has echolalia, which means she will often repeat the words or phrases of others, without considering the meaning of the words. Sometimes she has difficulty regulating herself, so you might see her doing movements like rocking or flicking her fingers as a way to calm herself when she's feeling anxious or stressed.

"But, along with the disabilities she has, Bethany has a number of unique things she's good at. One of them is being able to spell just about any name or word forward and backward instantly."

Now, this is just getting way too weird, I think to myself. I just want to walk into Mr. Rutter's office, close the door behind me and enjoy an hour of solitude.

"What's that noise? What's that noise? What's that noise?" Bethany repeats three times and begins rocking furiously back and forth once more.

I don't hear any noise but I'm beginning to feel distressed that she's freaking out so badly.

Suddenly, without warning, Bethany's arms shoot out and start grabbing eagerly at my lap. I can't tell if she's trying to hurt me or hug me, but I definitely don't like someone in my personal space. I attempt to brush her off me, using my shoulder to sort of put up a guard, but she swiftly reaches around the side of me until her hand rests on the paper butterfly sitting on my lap.

"Flap, flap, flap, make the noise again," she mumbles as she brings the butterfly to her own lap. I didn't realize it at the time, but I must have been squeezing the legs of the butterfly together absentmindedly when Bethany first sat down. It caused the wings to flap softly up and down, but it was so softly that I could barely hear it myself. How could that sound have bothered Bethany so much?

As if reading my mind, Mr. Rutter chimes in. "Because Bethany doesn't use sight to guide her, her other senses — including her hearing — are heightened. She's able to pick out individual instruments in an orchestra or hear the conversations of strangers in a crowded subway. It's quite astounding, actually. And she seems to be taken with your origami butterfly."

I look over and gasp as I watch Bethany begin to swiftly unfold my perfect creation until all that is left is a crumpled-up piece of paper.

Who does this girl think she is? I wonder, as rage starts bubbling up my spine. No one touches my origami pieces, not even if they ask. It has taken me hours to make that butterfly just perfectly so…and she goes and rips it from my hand to destroy it? I don't care what kind of disability this girl has. She has no right to walk in here and do this.

I feel tears stinging the backs of my eyes and I am about to reach over and grab the piece of paper back, when, as effortlessly as she has taken apart the butterfly, she proceeds to fold it up with impeccable precision, following the multiple steps required to perfection. Within an instant, my butterfly is back to its original form, its wings beating gently as Bethany squeezes the tiny legs again.

"How did you do that?" I manage to stammer. She continues to stare straight ahead, ignoring my question, just beating those wings with the same rhythm as when she had been rocking earlier.

"As I said," Mr. Rutter interrupts, "Bethany has abilities that many people don't understand. She is a very interesting girl, indeed."

He waves me forward as a signal that my office time with him will begin. As I follow him down the hall, my gaze is glued to Bethany sitting in that chair, softly humming something to herself now. Her mom has finished up the registration paperwork with the secretaries and casually walks over to Bethany. She speaks softly into her ear then guides her elbow up and leads her cautiously out into the bustling main atrium of the junior high. It isn't until they walk arm-in-arm past the wall of windows on the far side of the office that I realize Bethany is still cradling my butterfly delicately in her palm.

Chapter Seven

I'm such a book nerd that it should really be no surprise that language arts is my favorite class. I love diving into impossible worlds, going on adventures I never would have dreamed. It blows my mind that another human being can simply string a random set of words together in order to cultivate such vivid pictures in my mind that it feels as if I were in the book.

We're in the middle of doing a written response for *The Outsiders* — I know, ironic, right? — and I'm busy relating Ponyboy Curtis' character traits to my own. I find it interesting that practically every book we read has to do with a main character that doesn't fit in or who is the underdog in some way and has to overcome the odds. It's like they were all written for me. Maybe all authors are actually super-freaks who don't fit in, and they write books as a way of liberating themselves?

I look over at Kayla Sutton, undoubtedly the prettiest girl in our grade, and I wonder how in the world she is ever going to write this response. Long blonde hair, perfectly smooth skin, bright blue eyes... How could she possibly connect with an outsider? She is the definition of the 'inside'. Not surprisingly, her notebook appears to be totally empty. She holds her phone inconspicuously beneath her desk, and she is busy texting a mile a minute. So, there you have it. Kayla Sutton just can't do this assignment.

I find myself sometimes fantasizing about Kayla Sutton. Not in a weird, sexy way... I'm not into girls. Well, at least I don't really think so. At this point I'm not really into *anybody*. But I find that sometimes I can't stop staring at Kayla and wondering what it's like to be her. What would it be like to see people's faces light up every time you walk toward them in the hallway? To *be* good at everything you try, and to *look* good doing it, too. To see yourself in the mirror and genuinely love what you see. I would spend hours in front of the mirror if I were Kayla Sutton. I would brush my mane of silky hair until it shone in the sun. I would practice all the different expressions I could use to make people do pretty much anything I want—my cute pouty face, my brilliant million-dollar smile, my slight eyebrow arch of mock empathy.

Yes, being Kayla Sutton would be amazing. And the best part of it? Sean Fedun would be my boyfriend. If I were Kayla Sutton, the name Sean Fedun would no longer spark a burning ball of fire in my stomach, because he wouldn't bother me anymore. No, if I were Kayla Sutton, Sean Fedun would be putty in my hands. He would melt at my touch. I would smile coyly at him, looking up through sultry eyes, and he would wrap his arms around me, encircling me in his warmth. He would gently kiss my neck and I would get goosebumps as he crept his lips along my jaw.

Yeah, being Kayla Sutton would be the best. It would be everything that is the opposite of being me.

As I squint hard to catch a glimpse of any intimate texts that she might be sending Sean Fedun right now in the middle of language arts class, the door to the room opens. I look up, surprised to see Bethany Robertson walking in with a young woman in her twenties. Bethany is holding the young woman's arm, like she did with her mom, but she also has a white cane poised straight ahead, presumably to help her navigate the crowded classroom without tripping on the many desks and chairs. Ms. Kelly, our language arts teacher, stands up from her desk and walks to the door to chat with them for a few minutes.

She then turns, points her arm toward a little table near the back of the room and calls to get everyone's attention.

"Grade Nines, could I get your attention please? I have some people to introduce you to. This is Bethany Robertson. She transferred from John Franklin High. Bethany has some special needs, including autism and visual impairment, and so she works with Miss Karen, who is her educational assistant. Bethany is capable of a lot of the work we are all doing in class, but she needs Miss Karen's support to help her out. I trust all of you will be warm and welcoming to the both of them."

As they pass through the groups of desks spread out in the class, Miss Karen smiles widely and gives little waves to everyone she passes. Bethany's face remains neutral, her eyes flitting this way and that, impervious to the thirty pairs of eyes scrutinizing her every move. As they come closer to me, I take notice of how absolutely stunning Miss Karen is. She has smooth, golden skin the color of caramel, her hair hangs long and glossy black down her back, and her eyes sparkle wide and bright. She has a warm and inviting smile that is punctuated by two dimples positioned on each cheek. Her sense of style is bohemian and carefree — a long, flower-patterned summer dress with brown ankle boots and a large collection of golden bangles on one arm. Her ears are lined with a row of small gold-and-diamond piercings all the way to the top. And she has a tiny diamond stud in the side of her nose. She walks smoothly arm-in-arm with Bethany, navigating around chairs, book bags and gangly legs shooting out from desks. It's almost like watching a graceful gazelle leading an injured bird through the forest. All the kids stare at them with piqued attention. I'm unsure whether it is Bethany or Miss Karen who interests my classmates the most. They appear an unlikely pair as they finally make their way to the table at the back.

After they settle in, everyone gets back to work and the classroom quiets down. I feel a tap on my shoulder and turn to find Miss Karen beaming her movie-star smile at me.

"Excuse me. I was just wondering if you could help us out for a moment? I'm trying to figure out what page you guys are on so I can get Bethany caught up on her work?"

I'm perplexed for a moment, because I'm not sure what Miss Karen means. How is Bethany supposed to actually read the book? And I have to admit that part of me is sort of put out that she has asked for my help. Why doesn't she just ask one of the other kids in the class? I was happy in my own quiet little world at the back of the room and I feel annoyed by the disruption.

"Umm, well we're supposed to have read up to Chapter seven, but we're just working on a written response right now," I respond briskly.

"Oh, super! Bethany's just going to love this book. It used to be one of my favorites." She turns momentarily to open a large hardcover text with the words *The Outsiders* written on the front, but which looks far different from the paperbacks sitting on the rest of our desks. She whispers something into Bethany's ear and Bethany begins tracing her fingers along something inside the first page of the book.

"So, Bethany can read?" I blurt out absentmindedly. "I thought she couldn't see?"

"Oh yes, Bethany is blind, but, boy, does she love to read. She knows how to read braille and she's quite brilliant at it, actually. I'll make a guess that she'll have the entire book read by the end of the day." I glance over at Bethany, who is moving her finger so furiously across the page that I have a difficult time believing she is actually reading.

"And what's your name, hon?" Miss Karen turns back to me.

"That's Jodie McGavin. J-o-d-i-e-M-c-G-a-v-i-n. She makes butterflies. She gave me a butterfly," pipes in Bethany's robotic voice from behind the table. She holds the butterfly I'd made out in front of her and softly strokes the smooth wings as she gently rocks back and forth in her chair.

"Oh, you're the friend that Bethany made! She's been talking nonstop about you and the butterfly for the last two days. It's nice to meet you, Jodie." Miss Karen smiles and puts out her hand for me to shake.

Bethany's friend? What is she talking about? I literally just sat beside the girl as she practically pounced on me to get my origami art. Actually, she *stole* my origami art, so no, we are *not* friends. I don't even know this girl. And how in the world could she tell it's me? It's not like she can see me sitting here. Has she, like…memorized my voice? That is so creepy. I'm about to let Miss Karen know exactly how I feel about Bethany here stealing my stuff and stalking me when she starts up again.

"You know, it's really great that Bethany has met someone as cool as you already at this school. We had a lot of problems with other kids bullying her at her old school. I mean, I know she's really different and can be a lot to take, but they were really cruel to her. That's why we thought it was best to start fresh here at Maple Ridge. I can tell already we're both going to love it. Thanks again for reaching out and being the first to sort of welcome her.

"By the way, you can just call me Karen. It's always kind of weird to me when I get called Miss Karen, like I'm an old lady or something. I'm more of a big sister or a best friend to Bethany…and I want you to feel just as comfortable. I know we're all going to hit it off."

I don't know what to say. How did the seventh period turn into such a bizarre scenario? I was just sitting here doing my work, minding my own business, and now I'm supposed to be best friends with this nutcase? No thanks. I have enough trouble figuring things out on my own without having to babysit a special needs kid. She probably can't even hold a conversation. I mean, what would we even talk about? What could we possibly have in common? She can't even see! I imagine how I would look walking down the hallway holding her arm as kids laugh and throw paper snowballs at us. They would probably say that we're a couple or something. No, I have enough of my own problems and don't need someone else dragging me down further.

"Yeah, nice meeting you too...uh...Karen," I manage to stammer before I turn back to my writing piece. I had been in the middle of copying a quote from *The Outsiders* before my quiet bubble of solitude was unapologetically popped. As I look down at my page, I read the quote.

It seemed funny to me that the sunset she saw from her patio and the one I saw from the back steps was the same one. Maybe the two different worlds we lived in weren't so different. We saw the same sunset.

Through my peripheral vision, I see Bethany's finger running madly across the pages of her book and faintly, almost imperceptibly, I can make out the soft fluttering of the butterfly's wings as Bethany holds it in her lap. The buzzer sounds to mark the end of the day, and I've never been more eager to get home and into the solace of my room.

Chapter Eight

I'm still fuming as I bolt out of the school's main doors a few minutes later. My mom is supposed to pick me up for a doctor's appointment today so I'm looking for her silver SUV among the long line of cars idling in the parent parking lot.

As I walk down the front sidewalk, I laugh when I notice Anna and Amy repeatedly chasing each other up the side hill then taking turns rolling down. I remember doing that when I was little, and there was something so exciting about that dizzying tumble down a hill — the loss of all control, the boundless energy, the adrenaline rush of not knowing when or how you will stop, the freedom of not giving a crap who is watching.

I wonder why Mom doesn't have them strapped into their car seats, especially if we're in a rush to get going. But then I look over at her chatting with another mom I've never seen before. As I approach, I see Kayla Sutton walk up from the far side of the walkway.

"Hi there, sweetie," my mom chirps. "Look who I just happened to run into!" She makes this wild gesture toward the woman standing next to her, as if it clearly explains things.

"This is Donna Sutton! Donna and I used to dance together ages ago. Can you believe it? Our daughters have attended the same school for years and we didn't even know it. You know Kayla here, don't you?"

"Um, yeah. Hey, Kayla..." I mumble under my breath. I am keenly aware that those are the first two words I have ever uttered to Kayla Sutton in my entire life. We aren't exactly best friends. I can tell by the way Kayla is pulling on her mom's arm that she is feeling as awkward with this exchange as I am.

My mom catches the hint and starts to herd Amy and Anna into the back of our car. Then she turns and calls over her shoulder.

"Well, Donna, I think your idea is a brilliant one! I'll fill Jodie in on our way home. I can tell the twins are getting impatient, so we should probably get going, but it was really great to see you. I'd love to get together for coffee to catch up! We can talk more tomorrow, I suppose. I'll pick Jodie up from your place about nine, then?"

What is my mom talking about? She's picking me up from Kayla Sutton's house tomorrow? Hell no! I don't know what sort of crazy plan she has concocted, but I am not going along with it. I can tell Kayla is feeling the same way, because I see her shooting her mom a death stare before she slinks into the front seat of their truck. I follow her lead and slam the passenger door as I sulk as deeply as possible into the front seat of our vehicle.

Neither Mom nor I say a word to each other until the girls are buckled back into their car seats, *Paw Patrol* blasting on the iPad in front of them.

"What's going on? What did you do?" I demand.

"Oh, it was such a neat coincidence. And Kayla seems like such a lovely girl. I think you two are just going to hit it off tomorrow!"

She goes on to fill me in on the arrangements she has just made. Apparently, Mrs. Sutton and my mom ran into each other in the parking lot and got reminiscing about the old performances and competitions of their dancing days. Mrs. Sutton went on and on about how Kayla was following in her footsteps and that she was such an incredible dancer. Mom must have felt somewhat overshadowed, because she ended up making some crazy statement about how I always wanted to be a dancer too and wouldn't I love watching Kayla perform one day.

So, of course, Mrs. Sutton had to make use of any opportunity to parade her daughter's achievements even further. She suggested that I take the bus home from school with Kayla tomorrow, so we could hang out at her place for a while and 'catch up'. Then I could go and watch Kayla in the dance showcase she was performing in tomorrow night.

"But, Mom, I'm not even friends with Kayla Sutton! This is going to be so awkward."

"Well, is she a horrible person? Is there a reason you can't become her friend? A new friend is such a gift, Jodie!"

And it's true. Kayla has never been one of the kids who is outright rude to me. She just isn't anything to me. I'm pretty sure she didn't even know my name until my mom set this whole thing up.

"Mom, I'd rather just be by myself. I just like spending time alone."

"Jodie, it would be good for you to branch out a bit and spend some time out of your room. Everyone needs friends, and Kayla might just be the one to open you to a whole new social circle. I heard she's even tight with that cute boy Sean Fedun. Well, wouldn't it be a dream to get into *that* little clique?"

Yeah, my mom doesn't get me at all. I slowly come to terms with the fact that there is no way out of this situation. My heart palpitations start immediately, and I know they won't stop until tomorrow evening's dance fiasco comes to an end. And suddenly it dawns on me that I might find out exactly what it's like to be Kayla Sutton, whether I want to or not.

* * * *

I wade through the lessons of the next day as if I'm swimming in molasses. Sounds are deadened, nothing tastes right and my brain can't keep up with the most basic concepts in class. I just keep thinking about what's going to happen after school. How I'm going to deal with the massive undertaking before me.

There are just so many things to worry about, so many things that could go wrong. The entire day started out ass-backwards and I can't imagine it turning around.

First of all, I couldn't decide what to wear this morning. I don't want to look like I'm trying too hard and all of a sudden show up to school in something completely out of my character. But let's be honest. I wear sweats or leggings most days and it's kind of tough to make that look *en vogue*. I settled on a pair of jeans and a bright red top that kind of goes off the shoulder. It's not something I typically wear. In fact, I had to rip the tag off before I pulled it over my head this morning. My mom got it for me as part of my 'back-to-school shopping', seeing as I spent all my money on my new comforter. I guess she just can't let go of the fact that my sense of style is not worth saving.

I'm thankful that high-rise jeans are kind of in style right now, because it means that my muffin-top is sort of concealed and squished in. And the way the red blouse hangs, it sort of skims over my waist and hangs long in the back to cover my butt. Those are the two parts of me that are really not worth seeing up close. Sometimes I feel like I resemble the Kool-Aid man — all skinny legs and a big, round torso. Or maybe I'm a walking apple, like the candy apple on a stick you get from the fair. Clothes just don't fit me as well as I'd like.

In the top I've chosen to wear, there are two cut-outs at the shoulders, exposing my bare skin. Normally I would be horrified to expose any more of me than is absolutely necessary, but at least the cut-outs are at the tops of my shoulders where it's smooth and somewhat firm. The wobbly, dimpled bits of my upper arms are discreetly covered. I'm actually feeling like this outfit is maybe the best I've got. All my bad bits are camouflaged and the good-ish bits are highlighted. That's what fashion is all about, isn't it?

But after spending so much time scrutinizing my body, I had to look up and deal with the bigger problem — my insane hair. Granny Deans' voice kept going through my head. *'Pull it off your face, Jodie!'* So, I attempted to put it into a ponytail. I was successful at slicking it back at the sides and the top, but the ponytail itself is so thick and bushy that it looks more like a torpedo shooting out of the back of my head than a cute, loose-hanging pony.

And my makeup... Well, that's the problem. I don't wear makeup, whereas Kayla Sutton, being basically the ringleader of the sprites, wouldn't be caught dead without it. I rummaged through my mom's makeup bag this morning to find something to put on my face, but it was a useless venture. All my mom's makeup is made for a blonde-haired, blue-eyed, middle-aged mom, not a black, pimply-faced fifteen-year-old. I finally settled on a dab of lip gloss and left it at that.

Despite worrying about my looks, I've felt a lot of anxiety all day about what was even going to happen tonight. I didn't expect Kayla to suddenly become my best friend because of this, but I thought she'd at least smile at me in the hall or fill me in on the details. But she hasn't even made eye contact all day and we are now heading into last period. I kind of hope she'll drop the whole idea and we can both go our separate ways. But then I think of how disappointed my mom would be, how I would be failing her once again for not even trying.

But now I'm sitting here in last period and realize it all might be out of my hands altogether. I mean, Kayla hasn't spoken a word to me all day and we're supposed to head home together in under an hour. I think of the excuses I could give Mom. *Kayla is sick. I have a math test tomorrow and need to study. A hurricane plowed through the school and everyone got sent directly home...*

As I'm lost in my thoughts, I feel something softly knock against my shoulder and land on the desk in front of me. I look down and notice that it's a folded-up note, and I catch a glimpse of Kayla's swishy blonde hair swaying past me. Instead of feeling special that the most popular girl in our grade has just passed me a note, my heart sinks even further as I recognize she doesn't even want to be seen talking to me. I open the note, expecting to find a lame excuse why this evening's plans are canceled, but instead, there is just a simple sentence.

Meet me at the bus stop across from the school.

I have a really tough time concentrating for the remainder of language arts class, as I spend the entire period flip-flopping between berating myself for wearing a cheap pair of no-name jeans from Walmart and convincing myself of topics we could talk about during the long bus ride to her place.

The final bell eventually rings, and I walk to my locker to pack up my bag.

"Hey, Jodie, how are you?" I hear a sweet and friendly voice call to me. My heart skips a beat, thinking it's Kayla. Maybe she really is excited to have me come over? Maybe this will be the start of something good, like my mom suggested?

But when I look up, I see Miss Karen standing there with Bethany. Kayla is nowhere in sight.

"Oh, hi, Miss Karen. I mean…Karen. Hi, Bethany."

There's a long, awkward pause as Karen and I wait for Bethany to join in and say hi too, but she's too busy flicking her fingers against the side of my locker, seemingly oblivious to the fact that they were the ones who started a conversation with me.

"Um, what's up? Do you need something? I'm actually in a bit of a rush to get going. I'm going to be late catching the bus."

"Oh, well, Bethany and I were talking, and we were wondering if you'd like to hang out with us after school? On Wednesdays, we often go to this cool frozen yogurt place on the way home. We thought you might like to join us."

That's when Bethany finally joins in, as if the words 'frozen yogurt' make her come alive.

"Chocolate fudge with chocolate chips and sprinkles...but only on the side. Sprinkles always on the side. And it has to be a bowl. Not a cone. Never a cone. Always a bowl. Chocolate fudge in a bowl."

"Sorry... Bethany's a little particular about her frozen yogurt. She tends to like things the same all the time. Boring, if you ask me, but that's Bethany for you!" Karen again gives me that warm and confident smile that makes a person feel like there is no one else in the world she would rather be talking to.

"So, are you in? Do you want to join us?"

Well, this is a first. I've never in my life had two invitations in one day. Although, as my eyes flick toward Bethany, I feel more and more like this is just Karen's way of killing time with Bethany, and that Bethany really has no opinion about hanging out with me or anyone else. I wonder if Karen ever gets bored hanging out with Bethany? It doesn't really seem like Bethany can hold much of a conversation, and I wonder what they do together.

No. I am not interested in being anyone's babysitter. I suddenly feel a little insulted that Karen has asked me to be the one to hang out with them. I mean, just because I'm not the most popular kid in school doesn't give her the right to push the special needs girl on me. In fact, I'm starting to think that it's totally rude of her. She probably sought me out on day one—the one student dumb and lonely enough to actually buy her nice-girl act. She is planning on using *me* to make *her* job easier. *No way.* This is not how things are going to go down.

"Actually, I have plans with Kayla Sutton. You know who Kayla Sutton is, right? I'm, like, actually heading to her house right now. We're going to hang out for a while at her place, then she invited me to this totally cool dance showcase that she's in. It's going to be so awesome. So no, I can't hang out with you and Bethany." And I turn to close my locker with a flourish. I'm surprised to find that I say the entire monologue with a VSCO-girl cadence I didn't even know I was capable of. You would think the words came right out of the mouth of one of the sprites.

Karen is graceful with her response, but I can tell by the flicker in her eyes that she is surprised and maybe even a bit hurt.

"Oh, it's no problem, Jodie. You go have fun with Kayla. Maybe we can do it again some other time." She gives me a little wave and again beams her perfect smile. Then she puts her hand on Bethany's lower back and steers her away in the other direction. I can't hear what she whispers into Bethany's ear, but Bethany's response is loud and clear.

"Jodie McGavin doesn't like frozen yogurt? But I like frozen yogurt. Chocolate fudge with chocolate chips and sprinkles. But sprinkles on the side, Karen. Always sprinkles on the side. And in a bowl. Not a cone. Never a cone. Karen, don't let them put it in a cone."

"Yes, Bethany, I know. Sprinkles on the side and frozen yogurt in a bowl. And maybe Jodie McGavin will like frozen yogurt more next week. Come on. Let's go."

I feel a lump of guilt rising up my throat but quickly swallow it down. I have no reason to feel bad. After all, I have plans already and I am free to hang out with anyone I want. I glance up at the clock in the hall and realize that it's already a quarter after three. I hope that Kayla hasn't left without me. Funny how an hour ago I was dreading this meeting, but now I can't get there fast enough. Maybe Mom was right and it's time for my social circle to expand after all.

Chapter Nine

I try to walk with as much confidence as I can muster, but the trek to the bus stop across the street feels a million miles long. I see Kayla there with two of her friends, although I can't even think of their names because I'm so nervous. I think one of them might be the girl who passed me the elastic. Rebecca something, I think? I try not to stare, but I find that my gaze keeps veering back to the group of them. I suddenly feel intensely jealous — of their beauty, of their easy way of hanging out together, as if it's no big deal. Of the way their jeans fit perfectly around their butts and long, slender legs. Of the way their shirts graze just above their waists so that a sliver of skin is visible every time they turn or bend down. I immediately feel self-conscious about the off-the-shoulder shirt I picked out this morning and I'm acutely aware of a sharp pinching from the waistband of my jeans.

And I'm not the only one taking note of the girls. Surrounding them are a group of five or six boys drooling with every interaction. They remind me of dogs begging for scraps of food under the table. Even from a distance you can tell that they're eager to get the girls' attention. They laugh at every joke, they generously tease and flirt and they come up with all sorts of random reasons to touch or tickle each other. I don't think anyone has tickled me in my entire life. I wonder if I would even like it?

I notice that Sean Fedun is one of the boys in the group, which makes this task even more daunting. As I approach, he flicks his hair back, looking up at me, then elbows his buddy as if to say, "What's *she* doing here?"

"Uh, hi, Jodie." Kayla glances quickly in my direction then turns to her friends and stifles a giggle.

"Hi, Kayla. Um, your note said to meet you at the bus stop. We're still heading to your place, right? At least that's what my mom told me..." I say this with much more confidence than I feel.

The boys all look away...whether in embarrassment, disgust or lack of interest, I'm not sure. Kayla answers nonchalantly without looking me straight in the eye. "Yep. We're heading to my place. The bus should be here soon."

To say the next five minutes is awkward is an understatement. I'm not quite sure what to do with myself. I had prepped myself for having to make conversation with Kayla Sutton, and that was bad enough. But now I'm forced to be this strange addition to an obviously closed clique of friends.

The boys continue their teasing, and it doesn't go unnoticed by me that Sean finds a way to grab Kayla's hand or put his arm around her waist at least seven times during the short time we stand there. She pretends to be oblivious to his touch, although I can tell that's not the case as I see goosebumps prickle on her tanned forearms.

Every time I gain enough nerve to join in with what they are saying, the conversation abruptly changes and I'm left floundering, trying to think up something new. At some point, I resign myself into silence, praying that once the bus arrives, Kayla and I will be the only ones who get on and I can attempt to have a regular conversation with her.

A few more moments pass, then the bus finally pulls up. The boys give quick hugs, taking care not to miss any of the girls...well, except for me. I stand at the periphery of the circle, looking down at my sneakers to avoid any kind of eye contact. Sean Fedun is the last to say his goodbyes and, to my surprise, he puts his hand out to me for a high-five.

I'm caught off-guard but get my palm up to momentarily make contact with his. A little too loudly over his shoulder he calls out, "Have fun, ladies!" then smirks and joins his friends down the sidewalk. I can't decide if Sean Fedun's touch is a good omen or a bad one.

The three girls huddle themselves onto a couple of corner seats at the back of the bus, their backpacks resting on their laps. There is an empty space beside the one with the red hair — Zoe, maybe? — but I'm not sure whether it's meant for me or not. I pause momentarily in the middle of the aisle, when I hear Kayla call over to me.

"Jodie, come sit with us over here!" A wave of relief rushes over me, and I start thinking that maybe I've judged Kayla too harshly. Maybe she's open to including me after all.

I sit half-perched on the edge of the seat, acutely aware that the redhead has scooted herself as closely to the side of the bus as possible, so as to make room for me. I don't typically take the bus, and when I do, I always have a seat to myself. These seats are not made to comfortably seat two people, I think to myself in an effort to try to sit a little more naturally.

"Jodie, these are my friends, Zoe and Rebecca. Girls, this is Jodie, the one I was talking about?" There is a definite edge in Kayla's voice.

"Hi, Jodie, nice to meet you," Zoe squeaks out through giggles. I'm not sure what I've done that is so funny, so I just try to ignore her laugh. Out of the corner of my eye, I notice Rebecca looking at me solemnly and with empathetic eyes. She doesn't have the constant urge to giggle like the other girls. But when I dart my eyes over to her, she looks away quickly, as if she'll give away some hidden secret.

I notice a book peeking out from her backpack and recognize it instantly as one of my favorites. *The Glass Castle* by Jeannette Walls. I'm surprised, as I haven't seen many girls my age read something quite so powerful and real. Most of the girls are into vampire-plagued love stories or the latest graphic novel. Hell, half of the boys in my classes are still reading *Diary of a Wimpy Kid*.

I take a moment to capitalize on a rare shared interest and ask, "So, have you finished the book yet? It's one of my all-time favorites."

Rebecca starts to respond to me, but at the very same moment, Kayla starts talking and Rebecca's reply is immediately overshadowed.

"So, my mom says you like to dance, Jodie? I bet you're a great dancer. Which studio do you dance at again?" It's not difficult to hear the sarcasm in Kayla's voice and I'm not sure how to respond.

"I actually don't really dance myself. I just really love to watch it. I appreciate it as an art form, I g-guess," I stammer, my face starting to burn hot and no doubt red. Rebecca gives me an encouraging smile, but then Zoe jumps in.

"So, is it that you appreciate the dance form or you appreciate that the dancers are all wearing bodysuits and tights?" She looks at Kayla, as if to gain approval, then starts up again.

"We see you looking at us all the time, Jodie, and it's totally weird. Are you, like, into us or something?"

"Zoe!" Rebecca yells out, and smacks Zoe hard on the shoulder. "Leave her alone. She hasn't done anything wrong."

"Of course not. She can't help it if she's attracted to beautiful people!" At that, she flicks her long red hair over one shoulder as she and Kayla erupt into an explosion of giggles.

"But just so you know, Jodie, we're not into girls, so don't expect us to return the crush anytime soon. We are definitely boy-crazy!" The hysterics continue. "But I hear that Ms. Flanagan is into girls, so you could always ask her out if that's your thing."

Ms. Flanagan is our PE teacher and the senior girls' soccer coach. It's widespread knowledge that she's a lesbian, although she generally likes to keep her personal life private, for obvious reasons. The kids in our school seem to have a hard time accepting anyone who's different—be it staff or student. I feel like even more of an outcast than usual right now, and I'm not sure how to defend myself without coming off as either combative or discriminatory.

"Sorry. They don't mean that," Rebecca says quietly under her breath. She looks as if she wants to jump off the bus and I feel like I want to jump right off with her.

I look out of the window and realize I have no idea where I am. I try to catch a glimpse of a street sign, but they are zooming by too quickly. I am vaguely aware of the tall buildings of downtown to my right and the south mountains to my left, but the vast expanses of barren hills dotted with saguaro cacti do little to narrow down the neighborhood. All I know is that we've been on the bus for nearly a half-an-hour and it seems strange to me that Kayla's house would be so far away.

As if reading my thoughts, Kayla pipes up. "Oh, Jodie, we're just kidding. Can't you take a joke? That's what friends do. We tease each other. Don't worry. We're almost there. We'll get off at the next stop."

Kayla makes a big show of organizing her belongings and puts her jean jacket back on. She stands before the bus has even come to a stop and so I do the same. Since we're on the aisle side of the seat, we are the ones to lead the way to the door. Kayla insists I go first, so I press the button to open the door, and I walk down the three steps to the sidewalk.

"Oh, whoops, my shoelace is undone. I better stop to tie it up!" I hear Kayla's voice, still inside the bus. But when I turn around, she's not tying her shoelaces. She's not exiting the bus. She is standing in the middle of the aisle with her hands on her hips and an exaggerated pout on her lips.

"So sorry, Jodie. It looks like I've taken too long tying my shoe. I've gone and missed the stop and now I can't get off. We'll just have to do this little playdate thing another day. Be safe getting back home!"

The doors of the bus squeeze shut, but it doesn't do anything to block out the shrieks of laughter from inside. Kayla hurtles through the aisle, practically landing on Zoe's lap in a heap of giggles. The bus's exhaust pipe lets out a low grumble and it slowly peels away from the curb. Rebecca catches my eye and I think I see her mouth the words *I'm sorry*, before I crumble into a pile of tears.

I have no idea where I am. The neighborhood is not one I'm familiar with, so I reason that I must be on the far side of the city. I remember crossing the Salt River and passing the outskirts of downtown Phoenix about twenty minutes into the ride, which means I must be somewhere in the southwest part of the city — all the way across town from my house in the upscale suburban area of Scottsdale. I immediately conclude that walking home is not an option. I pull out my phone and start dialing my mom's number, but stuff it back in my pocket before I've even hit *send*.

How is calling Mom going to help with this situation? My mom is the last person I want to talk to right now. My mom is the one who caused this whole catastrophe to happen. She is so eager to have me accepted by others that she just can't accept me herself.

I can't believe I even went along with her suggestion. How stupid am I to think those girls would ever want to hang out with me? How stupid am I to even want to hang out with them? But then I think of Rebecca's kind eyes and quiet apology. I think of the book she's reading and the possibility that there's more to her than I would have expected. But I guess she's having a tough time being herself too.

I decide the best thing to do is to wait for another bus to come. Surely if a bus dropped me off here, another would come to take me back to school? From there I'm not sure what to do. My mom is supposed to be picking me up from Kayla's house in five hours. I can't let her know about this. I will never tell her about this humiliating event. No, I'm better off just killing time all evening then making up some story about how Kayla's parents were kind enough to drop me off after the show. I just hope my mom won't be going for coffee any time soon with Mrs. Sutton, where she can find out the truth.

An hour and a half after I was deserted across town like a piece of garbage on the side of the road, I finally get off a different bus at the stop down the street from my house. All I want to do is grab a bag of popcorn and a giant glass of iced tea and hole myself up in my room. I hate thinking that I still need to wait another three hours before I can go home. I start thinking about all the excuses I could make up for why I'm home so early. Maybe I can say Kayla wasn't feeling well so she decided not to dance in the showcase after all? Or maybe I can blame it on not feeling well myself. Period cramps always worked in the past, but since 'the incident', the thought of using my period for any type of story makes me sick. I don't want to have to relive any part of that.

But really, what am I thinking? I can't go home. It'll be like walking into a firing squad of questions that I'm going to have to shield with an arsenal of lies. No…better to just wait this one out. I turn in to the strip mall down the street from our place and decide to spend a bit of time with a long-forgotten friend.

The library.

I realize that it's kind of weird for me to love the library this much. Most kids my age spend so much time on electronics that they haven't ever opened a book that wasn't a school assignment. But not me. I adore the library — the musty book smell, the aisles upon aisles of untapped adventures, all organized with the utmost accuracy. The way a person can just disappear between the stacks without anyone asking questions. The fact that talking is not only discouraged but frowned upon. Even the clientele of the library puts me at ease. It's mostly filled with aging grannies napping on the side couches or tiny toddlers with their nannies in tow, hoping to make it for the *Sing, Laugh and Read with Me* group.

Then there's me. I can wander at my leisure and spend as long as I'd like, vanish into a thousand other worlds. To tell you the truth, my favorite thing to do in the library is choose a new origami creation to start and zone out by myself until I've mastered it.

I've got a couple of new books on origami that I've recently put on hold, so I head to the front desk to take them out before I do anything. Then I carry the towering pile to my special spot at the back corner of the room. It's sandwiched between the aisle on ancient civilizations and the one on aerospace, and hardly anyone comes down this way. There's a ratty old sling-back chair here, with a little coffee table on one side and a small aluminum garbage can on the other. I swear no one but me uses this area, and it's free every time I come. I once accidentally left a piece of chewing gum on the table beside a can of Coke I had been drinking. When I came back to the library three days later, it was still sitting there, all hard and rubbery, already collecting a thin layer of dust.

I reach my cozy spot in the corner, away from the old man who is constantly coughing up phlegm into his handkerchief, away from the preschoolers using the bookshelves as a make-believe maze, away from the cruelty of fifteen-year-old girls.

I'm really excited about this one new origami book I've been waiting on. There aren't that many origami books out there that I haven't already combed through, and I've completed all the simple projects a dozen times. This book is super-cool because it's Harry Potter-based, so there are directions on how to make intricate paper versions of just about everything in the book series. Obviously, there are directions on how to make the owls, wands, broomsticks and dragons, but one section of the book details how to make the entire scene of Diagon Alley, and another Chapter goes through a step-by-step guide on how to create a paper replica of Hogwarts. I've already cleared off an entire shelf in my room to build my miniature Harry Potter world.

I pick up the first sheet of crisp white paper from my pile and I begin. I'm so glad I've decided to pop in here before making my way home. The reading and folding has a calming effect on me and I'm feeling a lot less upset about the episode with Kayla and her friends — like it was a really bad dream from last night, and the details of it are starting to fade just a bit.

Chapter Ten

I'm immersed in my own world of witchcraft and castles when I hear someone stride over to me. For a split second I worry that Kayla and her friends have found me here and are going to make fun of me for doing something as lame as origami. Then, before, I suddenly panic, thinking it's my mom and that maybe Mrs. Sutton has filled her in on the entire event.

But I needn't have worried, because when I look up, I see Miss Karen's smiling face, with Bethany patiently standing beside her.

"Hey, Jodie, what are you doing here? Didn't you have an event planned tonight with Kayla?"

Oh geez, even the special-needs kid and her aide are witness to the massive embarrassment of being catastrophically ditched.

"Um, yeah, I did. But Kayla wasn't feeling great, so we decided we'd just do it another day. I had a few books on hold so I thought I would pop in here before heading home. Weren't you guys supposed to be going out for ice cream?" I add, as if to challenge whether they had bent the truth too.

"Yeah, we already did that. Usually, I just take Bethany home afterward, as my shift is done at four-thirty, but Bethany's parents asked me to stay a little later tonight as they've got a dinner planned with friends. So, we thought we'd check to see if her new braille books are in yet."

"So, how exactly does it work with Bethany? You get paid to just hang out with her? Isn't that weird?"

"Well, I don't get paid to hang out with her exactly. I mean, at school I'm her educational assistant, so I act as a sort of translator for the teachers. But I've known the family for so long that sometimes I just help Bethany's parents out by spending time with her so they don't get so burned out. As awesome as Bethany is, it can be pretty exhausting being the parent of a special-needs kid."

She reaches over and squeezes Bethany's hand as she says this, and Bethany responds with an awkward smile and continues to flick her fingers together repeatedly.

"So, you said that you have known Bethany for a long time. How did you even get working with her?"

"Well, I used to work as a camp counselor in the summers at a camp designed for kids with special needs. Bethany started coming when she was about eight, the same year I started out as a junior counselor. She was the sweetest little thing with these super-cute curly pigtails and this incredible giggle. And boy, was she ever smart. To this day, Bethany knows things that I'll never be able to figure out. She's just such an incredible girl. We hit it off right from the start, and so we looked forward to seeing each other every summer.

Eventually I graduated from high school, got my diploma in special ed, and three years ago was hired as her EA. Now we spend every day together and she is literally like my little sister."

"But how do you have like...a relationship with her? Does she even talk with you? And what do you guys actually do together?" I'm aware of the fact that I sound judgy, but it just doesn't make sense to me. It just seems like Bethany is in her own world most of the time.

"Like everybody, Bethany is a little shy and standoffish when she first meets someone. But if you put the effort into getting to know her, it really pays off. She is one of the coolest people I know."

I look at Karen with her exotic beauty, her bohemian 'I don't give a shit what anyone thinks of me' style, and I am in awe. I wish I could be so carefree, so confident. I wish I were Miss Karen.

"I just have to run to the washroom. Are you okay sitting with Bethany for a few minutes, Jodie?" Karen is standing before I even have a moment to respond.

"Oh, s-sure. No p-problem," I stutter, and I watch Karen walk down the nearest aisle. For a moment, I'm awkwardly paralyzed. I feel the need to start a conversation, but I can't think of anything to say. Surprisingly, Bethany is the one to break the silence.

"Jodie McGavin, J-o-d-i-e-M-c-G-a-v-i-n, Jodie McGavin. Spelled backward is n-i-v-a-G-c-M-e-i-d-o-J."

I can't help but laugh as I remember Bethany saying this exact line the first time we met.

"Yes, Bethany, you're right. So I guess you are Bethany Robertson. Umm-m, that would be B-e-t-h-a-n-y-R-o-b-e-r-t-s-o-n, backward it's n-o-s-t-r-e-b-b-o-R-y-n-a-h-t-e-B?"

Bethany explodes into a fit of laughter before blurting out, "Jodie, you said two b's! There aren't two b's. There's only one b!" She continues to laugh so hard that her cheeks flush and her chair rocks back and forth. I can't help but notice that she has two perfect dimples on her cheeks and she has possibly the whitest teeth I've ever seen. She has a small smattering of freckles across the bridge of her nose that gives her an innocence not common among most fifteen-year-olds. As she laughs, she does this high-pitched hiccup thing that makes me start to laugh too. I notice that every time she gets really excited or happy about something, her fingers start to flick each other again and it reminds me of my butterfly she was playing with the other week.

"Hey, Bethany, do you want to learn how to make a butterfly, like the one I gave you before? That way, you can flap the wings anytime you'd like."

"Yes, I like butterflies, Jodie McGavin. I love butterflies. Did you know there are seventeen thousand five hundred species of butterflies in the world? And the Palos Verdes Blue is the rarest. It lives in California."

I reach over to slide one of the blank pieces of paper under her restless hands. She immediately glides her fingers over it. Back and forth, back and forth, always with a similar repetitive rhythm.

"Okay, so, Bethany, you start by folding this corner into the center like this."

I begin coaching her through the steps, every so often guiding her fingers to mimic the directions I give her orally. I find that I have to be extremely explicit in my instructions, seeing as Bethany can't see any demonstrations I might want to give. I find it oddly satisfying talking Bethany through the task. She catches on incredibly quickly and I am impressed at the nimbleness and quickness of her fingers. Within minutes, a perfect replica of my butterfly is created.

"Wow, you guys have been busy while I've been gone. Sorry, Jodie. Bethany's mom called to check in, so I was chatting with her for a while. What are you guys up to?"

"Karen, Jodie is a really funny girl. She was making me laugh and laugh. And we made a butterfly. Not a real butterfly like the Palos Verde Blue. That butterfly is almost extinct. No one even sees the Palos Verde Blue. But I can make a paper butterfly. Watch me make a paper butterfly."

In an instant, Bethany grabs another piece of paper and deftly folds it, following the precise guidelines I gave her moments before. I hear her repeating the instructions I gave her word for word under her breath. Without missing a single step, she creates another replica butterfly in just minutes. It's hard for me to believe that her memory is so precise.

"Wow, Bethany. It's incredible you can remember that. It took me an entire afternoon to get that one right."

Bethany beams her dimpled smile, despite the absent gaze of her wandering eyes, and places the butterfly in the palm of my hand.

"Here, Jodie. It's a Palos Verde Blue butterfly. It's almost extinct, so you better put it in your collection. The real ones live in California. But, Jodie, this one isn't real. It's not alive. And I can make another one too. So, it's not really extinct. It's just paper."

"Thanks, Bethany. I have the perfect place to keep it," I reply, and I'm surprised to find I'm feeling a bit of excitement about being given a gift for my special shelf. It's been a long time since anyone gave me a gift — well, other than my parents or Santa Claus, that is. But no one is allowed to count those.

With a slight hesitation, I start packing up all my stuff.

"I better be going. Thanks for, um…hanging out. See you at school tomorrow."

"Actually, we're just heading out too, so we'll walk out with you. Let me just grab our stuff." Karen passes Bethany her cane and piles the braille books in her arm. She goes to reach for Bethany's elbow but it's a bit awkward because it leaves the pile of books teetering on her forearm.

My hands are free since I've put my backpack on, so I reach out, link my right arm through the crook of Bethany's elbow and slowly start leading her through the aisle. I didn't think about it when I did it. It was just sort of a reaction, like how you automatically hold the door open for an older lady who is coming through at the same time as you. But now that I feel the weight of her arm resting on mine and am cognizant of the unison of our footsteps, it all of a sudden feels very weird.

A swirl of thoughts and worries fills my brain. *Am I supposed to make conversation with her as we walk? How will I know if I'm going too fast? What happens when we get to the door? Do I push it open then tell Bethany to walk through or do I go first and hope she follows?*

It seems silly for me to have these thoughts, but those are the kinds of things that fill up my brain most days. I can't help it. It's like every social interaction I make is under a microscope, and things are magnified to the point that I can't even see what I'm doing anymore.

But nothing about Bethany's behavior leads me to believe she's sensing my awkwardness at all. She doesn't feel the need to fill the silence between us. She naturally keeps the same pace with me, and when we get to the main door—an automatic one, miraculously—she simply walks through without hesitation. There is so much trust in her that I will take her safely to where she needs to go. The entire five-minute adventure feels almost well...*normal*.

We stand outside in the early evening twilight, the heat of the day finally letting up. I say another goodbye and pass Bethany over to Karen so they can walk back to her house. I turn in the direction of my own house and literally smack straight into someone walking toward me on the sidewalk.

"Oh, sorry, I wasn't p-paying attention," I stammer in my usual self-deprecating way. I look up and find my gaze meeting the eyes of a tall, slender boy my age. He looks super-familiar, but I can't think of where I know him from until I glance down and lock in on his *Hi, I'm Jared* nametag.

"Hey, no worries. I wasn't really paying attention either." He pauses for a moment, as if I'm a puzzle he's trying to sort out.

"Wait... I know you from somewhere, don't I?" he questions.

I know exactly where I know him from, but there's no way I'm admitting to him that I'm the delinquent who spent half the afternoon skipping school at his frozen yogurt store because my period leaked all over the place to crown me as the biggest loser of ninth grade.

Nope, that wouldn't be the way to go. Better to just keep that to myself and hope he doesn't remember every single customer that comes through the door.

No such luck.

"Oh yeah, I remember now. You came into the store I work in. It was the middle of the day. I remember because you have that super-funky hair, and you were reading Stephen King."

Huh? He remembers my *hair* and what I was reading? And what did he say? *'You have that super-funky hair?'* Is that even a good thing?

"Um, I just don't remember. Sorry…" I am keenly aware once more how bad I am at lying.

"Remember? We were joking around about being dropouts? Because you were sick that day and I was working, even though it was a Wednesday. You ordered chocolate on a cone with gummy bears and hot fudge. Remember?"

He remembers what I ordered? How do I even respond to that? My first instinct is to think he's a bit of a creep, but a tickly feeling in my gut is telling otherwise. *He thinks I have funky hair…* No one has ever said anything nice about my hair. *Ever.*

I decide to give it a shot.

"Oh, right. I do remember you! You work at the frozen yogurt place, right? You're the homeschooled guy?" I immediately resent that last question coming from my mouth because I know it comes across all judgy. Inside my brain, the memory of Kayla flirting with all the boys floats past and I chastise myself. *Is this flirting? Is what I'm doing supposed to count as flirting? God, I'm terrible at this.*

Hi, I'm Jared seems totally unfazed by my comment and just continues.

"Well, in case you forgot, I'm Jared. I actually just got off work, so I'm heading home. What are you up to?"

"Um, I was just at the library with some friends and I'm heading home now too." I am desperately wanting the comfort of Bethany and Karen right now, just to ease the awkwardness of this disastrous conversation.

"Which way are you walking, because I live just down on Edison Street. If you're heading that way too, I could maybe walk with you?"

A small wave of panic passes through me, knowing I'm going to have to fill the entire twenty minutes' walk with conversation that I'm terrible at. But that tickly feeling in my stomach becomes more pronounced and I find that it outweighs the nerves.

"Uh, sure. I hate walking around when it's getting late, and it's already pretty dark out. It's still staying pretty warm in the evenings, though. That time of year, I guess."

Seriously, the weather? I resort to talking about the weather.

"I have a great idea. I'll pop back into the store and grab us each a cone to take on the road. Janine is closing tonight, and she won't care if I help myself to a couple of extras. Just wait here a minute."

I literally just stand there for five minutes, not knowing what to do. I pull out my phone as a distraction, but I don't want Jared thinking I'm one of those social-media-obsessed girls. I remember the lip gloss that I threw in my backpack this morning and hastily smother a bit on, using the reflective glass in the storefront as my mirror. I can just make out a tinted and blurry version of myself, and I am disheartened by what I see.

My hair is still slicked in that backward torpedo ponytail, and my face is shiny with grease and sweat after being out all day long. I'm thankful that I at least chose a half-decent outfit to wear this morning, anticipating my date with Kayla.

God, that memory feels like ages ago. Some of my anger and embarrassment has dissipated for the moment, and I'm grateful that Jared has provided a distraction.

A moment later he comes out with two heaping cones, mine complete with chocolate chips, hot fudge and gummy bears, just like I ordered that day a few weeks ago. I tell myself that he must just have some sort of crazy memory or something, but it still makes me feel good to think that he paid attention enough to remember. That someone was paying attention to *me*.

We walk in silence for a bit, me grateful for the cone so that my mouth is busy doing something other than talking. Then he asks me about the Stephen King book I was reading — again, he remembered! — and we get talking about favorite authors. The conversation turns again and he's asking me about school.

"Yeah, I go to Maple Ridge. It's okay, I guess. The teachers are pretty good and it's close to home..." I trail off, knowing how pathetic it is that the only good things I can recall from high school are the teachers and its proximity to my house.

"I wonder about high school sometimes. You know, whether I'm missing out on anything. I've been homeschooled for so long that I don't even know what a real school is like. Is it like the movies? Where the football players walk around the halls like they own the place, with the pretty cheerleaders at their sides?" He laughs when he says it, but he doesn't know how close to the truth he actually is.

"Well, why are you homeschooled anyway? Is your mom a hippie and wants you to resist current societal institutions?" I nudge him with my elbow, so he knows I'm just teasing, then I realize... I'm actually teasing a boy! I'm flirting and teasing at the same time. This might be too much to take.

"Everyone thinks that. I guess there are some homeschoolers out there like that—but not me. I guess my mom decided to homeschool out of convenience. I have a brother who is three years older than me and he has cerebral palsy. He needs a lot of support in his day-to-day functioning, never mind schooling. So, when he was born, my mom quit her job to look after him full-time. When he got to be school-age, his days were so full of OT, PT, SLP and doctor appointments that school became almost impossible. So, she decided to homeschool. I came along and it was just a no-brainer that I would stay at home with her and she would teach the both of us, while enabling Cal—that's my brother's name—to have all his therapist visits at our place."

Oh, wow. I didn't think he was going to say all that. For a split second I almost feel bad for Jared for not being able to experience school like the rest of us. Then I remember how nightmarish public school actually is for me.

"Trust me... You aren't missing anything. I'd do anything *not* to have to go to a regular high school."

We stop outside my place as I crunch the last bite of my waffle cone. I find a way to say a not entirely awkward goodbye by thanking him for the cone and giving him a little wave. In my books, it's a triumph that I've made it all the way home without so much as a stutter. He gives a little wave too and calls out that he hopes to see me around. I can't tell whether that's just teenage lingo for goodbye, or whether he actually hopes to see me around. Either way, I'm feeling noticeably lighter as I walk the way up my front steps, despite the fact that there's an entire pint of chocolate ice cream settling in my belly.

Chapter Eleven

It's the first Tuesday of the month. And as much as I typically look forward to Tuesdays because I get some one-on-one time with Mr. Rutter, I dread the first Tuesday of the month.

On the first Tuesday of the month, my mom is called into the school and the two of us have a joint session with Mr. Rutter to discuss my *progress*. Progress with what, I'm not sure. It's not like we have some sort of end goal in sight—"Jodie McGavin is going to be the most popular kid in ninth grade!"

No, high school just keeps ticking on and on and the only end goal will be when it's over in June. But I suppose it's in Mr. Rutter's job expectation that we are on the same page, and he somehow needs to communicate this to my mom. *Lucky me.*

Most of the sessions with my mom follow the same pattern. Mr. Rutter starts off by telling my mom about how great I'm doing in some random aspect of my schooling—like how I participated in PE class and I am now able to sprint a hundred yards! *Really?* Or how my latest project on photosynthesis is just outstanding and I should be so proud of myself. *Seriously. That* was *the big accomplishment of the year last term.* And I'm usually okay with him talking about academics, because…well, that's never really been a huge problem for me. I always do okay with school. Not stellar, but I get by.

I remember my dad saying once that he always aimed for a seventy percent in school. My mom was horrified when he said that because she has always been a self-professed overachiever, but he stood by his belief that a seventy percent was a perfect grade to attain. He said if you got lower than that, people might think you were stupid or you might be placed in one of those special ed classes with an adapted curriculum. He said if you got much higher than that — say in the eighties or nineties — you could be seen as a show-off and people would be irritated by you. Plus, he said then you'd be forced to enroll in the AP classes in high school, where you'd have to work twice as hard but get way worse marks and be with all of the other brainiacs you never wanted to hang out with anyway. Yep, to him seventy percent was right about perfect.

So, I guess that, in my dad's eyes, I hit the mark perfectly with my completely underwhelming GPA. But my mom always likes to check in with Mr. Rutter anyway on this aspect of my schooling. And Mr. Rutter always placates her by mentioning my academic achievements before jumping into his *pièce de résistance*, my social awkwardness.

"So how has Jodie been fitting in at school lately?" my mom invariably asks, once my grades have been dissected. Over the course of the last few weeks, Mr. Rutter has been trying to get me to step out of my comfort zone and make new friends. My mom has been so completely on board with his plan of action that she has been constantly peppering me with questions about what group I am working on a certain project with or whether there is anyone I want to have over for a sleepover. I think that's why she was so eager to set up that 'play date' with Kayla Sutton a few weeks ago. I know she wants more details about how it went, and I've been able to put her off up until this point. I got away with simple yes and no responses and I avoided telling her about the horrid details of being left on the side of the curb like trash. I know she's not ready to hear that. She wants to hear about how I have plans to meet friends at the mall after school — or that I've been assigned one of the lead roles in the school play and now my weekends will be busy with rehearsals. I know she sees Kayla Sutton as my easy ticket out of loneliness.

Her intentions are truly good. I know my mom loves me and just wants to ensure that I'm happy. But her version of happy differs vastly from mine, and she just can't seem to get that.

My mom is a super-outgoing, extroverted person who loves hosting parties, going out with large groups of friends and generally being the star of the show. I'm pretty sure she would have been one of the sprites, if that even existed when she was a teenager. Geez, she would have been the ringleader. I've seen pictures of her when she was younger, with her long, tanned legs, her silky blonde hair and sparkling blue eyes... Yeah, popularity would have been a contest made for her.

So, I get it that she wants me to fit in too. But there are some things that just get worse with a mom's constant meddling.

"Mr. Rutter, did Jodie tell you about her amazing get-together a couple weeks back? Kayla Sutton invited her over with a few friends and they all went to a dance showcase together."

It always sounds weird to me when my mom refers to my teachers by their last names, like she still thinks she's a student in high school or something. Or maybe she thinks it's a sign of respect? I hope I'm not in my forties still calling other men my age 'Mister'. Mind you, Mr. Rutter's first name is Eugene, so it could be that she just doesn't want to have to say that out loud. 'Eugene' sounds perverted and pathetic all at the same time—no offense to Mr. Rutter.

"No, Jodie, you didn't mention that. Why don't you tell me about it now?" Mr. Rutter looks at me with softness in his eyes.

"Well, it was no big deal. She just invited me to this dance thing." I am trying my very best to be honest without having to give away the exact details of what happened. I really suck at lying.

"Jodie, tell Mr. Rutter what you did and how you had such an amazing time!" I can hardly stand the eagerness in my mom's voice.

"Yeah, we hung out for a bit. It was great." This room suddenly feels very hot and stifling.

Mr. Rutter looks me in the eye, and I notice an almost imperceptible arch to his eyebrow, as if he's asking me in what direction I want this conversation to go. I don't have to say anything back to him. He can obviously guess by my downcast eyes and reddened face that the entire engagement with Kayla was a joke and that I have no interest in pursuing that friendship any further. It's so crazy for me to think that this short, nerdy middle-aged man reads my mind better than my own mother.

"You know, Mrs. Sutton, I've really noticed Jodie taking a leadership role in school lately. We have a new special-needs student who has registered at our school, and Jodie has been instrumental in stepping up and welcoming her."

"Really, Jodie? You didn't mention that at all! That sounds wonderful. Is there a group of you and some friends who are taking this on as a little project? Like a leadership club thing or something?"

"Well no, it's not really like that. I'm just... She's just..."

Mr. Rutter interjects. "Bethany has taken a liking to Jodie, and Jodie has really stepped up. It takes a lot of courage to befriend someone who is different. I've been really proud of her."

"Well, I'm glad to see that Jodie is helping out and it's great to see that she's showing leadership skills. But I'm not sure how comfortable I am with our focus being on her helping out a special-needs child? I mean, haven't we been pushing for her to branch out and get some real friends? This all feels a little, well...counter-productive to our goals for Jodie."

I see Mr. Rutter shift uneasily in his seat. I find that I'm teetering between two sides as I sit in on this meeting. I know my mom is looking out for my best interests, and she just doesn't see my relationship with Bethany as helping me climb the social ladder of ninth grade. And, to tell the truth, I'm not sure what to call my relationship with her, either. I mean, I just spend a few minutes with her in the library one day, and now, what? I'm her best friend or something? Ever since the day Kayla ditched me, Bethany and Karen have come to chat with me at my locker. They've asked to sit with me at lunch as well, but I keep making excuses about having to see Ms. Kelly about a language arts assignment. To tell the truth, I'm not sure how I feel about Bethany myself.

There's something about her that I find kind of intriguing, like when you read the first few pages of a lengthy new book. It might grab you and pull you in, but you always have to debate whether the story is strong enough and will be worth the effort to get through.

Choosing Bethany is basically the same thing as not choosing everyone else — or at least that's how my mom sees it.

"Well, why don't we see how things play out over the next few weeks and we can talk to Jodie about how she's feeling at that time? Jodie, does that sound reasonable to you?"

I notice that this is the first time I have been spoken to and not spoken about during this entire meeting.

"Sure, that sounds good. We'll just play it by ear." My mom takes a few moments to thank Mr. Rutter again for his time then we walk together out of the office door.

Before we part ways, my mom turns to me and speaks.

"Jodie, I don't want you to think that I'm callous or uncaring. I really do think it's wonderful that you've reached out and are helping another student in need. But do you really see this friendship going anywhere? I mean, does she give anything to you in return? Maybe you should focus on putting your efforts toward some of the other girls who are a little more like you? You know, find some kindred spirits?" As she says this last line, she nods over to a small group of girls in the corner who are laughing and playing on their phones.

I see what makes my mom so envious. There is just such ease between these girls. They sit closely, one girl making a tiny braid with another's hair. They are all dressed similarly, and the flow of conversation among them ripples like water bubbling through a quick-moving brook. Everything is effortless, like they are just being themselves. It's like these girls have found their tribe and I start to wonder whether I will ever find mine.

Chapter Twelve

After yesterday's meeting with my mom and Mr. Rutter, I'm left feeling more frustrated and isolated than ever before. Why does everyone feel the need to control my life? I mean, it's not like I'm depressed or suicidal. I don't get in trouble at school and I'm not on drugs or having sex. God, I haven't ever even kissed a boy or smoked a cigarette! Why can't everybody just leave me alone?

So what if I don't have a ton of friends? I don't understand why that's a problem. Aren't introverted people just allowed to be, well...introverted? So now I have to go about my days actually thinking about what I'm doing and who I'm talking to, like I'm on some weird friendship quest. *Talk to this person and you gain access to a special new world. Talk to that person and you sink to the pit of despair.* What is this epic consequence shit? I'm just trying to survive the ninth grade.

Since being abandoned by Kayla, she hasn't even cast a glance my way. I see Sean whisper and snicker at me every so often, so I'm guessing he might have been the ringleader of the whole prank in the first place, which really does make the most sense. Maybe those two deserve each other more than I used to think.

I've just sat down early in language arts class and I notice Kayla isn't here today. Sean is missing too, so my guess is that they ditched class together to hang out. Rebecca walks in on her own and hesitates for a moment before taking a seat next to me. I do my best not to look up. I don't want her thinking that I notice her at all. I don't want her to think that I care. Although I remember her mouthing the words *'I'm sorry'* on the bus and I soften toward her just a bit.

"So, I read it," Rebecca whispers softly, without even glancing toward me.

"Huh? Sorry… W-what was that?" I stammer.

"The Glass Castle. I just finished reading it. You know, the book you mentioned? It was really good. I just thought… I don't know. I just thought you might like to know."

I am blown away by the fact that Rebecca Sherman is talking to *me*. No, let me clarify. Rebecca Sherman *started* a conversation with me about a book I recommended to *her*. *What's going on here?*

Then I take note again that Kayla is absent from the picture. It deflates my enthusiasm just a little, as I know this exchange of words would not be happening if Kayla were here. But I gather my confidence and proceed anyway.

"Well, if you liked that book, you should try *Educated*. It makes *The Glass Castle* look like Disneyland. Some really crazy stuff. This girl basically grows up in the middle of the wilderness with nothing but a family that is totally insane. And it's a memoir too, so it's all true. I just don't get how some people can live with crazy families like that."

Rebecca nods and leans in to me as I speak, like she's trying hard to capture every word. We talk for at least ten minutes before Ms. Kelly starts the class and we need to end the conversation. But I'm relieved to find our exchange so effortless. I don't stumble on my words. I don't say the wrong things at the wrong time. I feel almost normal chatting with Rebecca, like we've been friends for ages.

As Ms. Kelly drones on about the next novel study we're going to do, I can't help but sneak glimpses of Rebecca from the corner of my eye. Maybe someone like her would like to hang out with someone like me. Is it so hard for me to imagine?

About a half-hour into class, I ask to be excused so I can grab my water bottle from my locker. There's a hallway off to the left of the classroom that is a new extension to the school. Enrollment has gone up so quickly over the past couple of years that they had to add more lockers and a couple of bathrooms. This is the hallway that houses my locker, and I'm good with it being a little out of the way. Only a dozen or so students use the lockers here, as they're usually saved for the new kids that come. It means this hallway is typically vacant and quiet, especially during class time.

But today, I hear noises coming from one of the bathrooms. When the renos were being done in this hallway, our school chose to put in gender-neutral bathrooms. I think it's meant to support inclusion and all that, but in reality, it has been used more as a make-out area for kids who want to cut class. The bathrooms are all made of private stalls with locked doors, so it's relatively easy to tuck yourselves away without being caught by the teachers.

I try not to eavesdrop as I shuffle through my backpack trying to locate my water bottle, but I can't help but be curious. The bathroom itself opens directly to the hallway, so the sinks are visible as you walk by. There are three private stalls with the doors wide open, and one stall with the door closed. I hear giggling and rustling happening in the one stall that's closed, so I crane my neck into the doorway of the bathroom to get a better sense of what's going on.

The bathroom doors don't extend all the way up to the ceiling or down to the floor, so there is a bit of space where you can see if someone is inside. A ribbon of pale gray smoke drifts up and over the door that's closed, and I smell the pungent stench of weed. I have no idea how kids can smoke that stuff, as it just reeks like a skunk to me.

Underneath the door, I make out two pairs of shoes. One, a pair of Converse Chuck Taylor high-tops and the other a pair of sparkly gold flip-flops—one girl and one boy. Well, no surprise there. The feet are facing each other and are very close together. The whispering has stopped, and in between the sound of crisp inhales, I hear the squishy, slobbery sounds of kissing. It makes me think back to when Kayla and her friends were flirting with the boys and they were tickling each other. I wonder whether I'll ever get to kiss a boy. How will it feel? Will I like it? How will he taste?

I would never admit it to anyone, but just last week I tried to French kiss myself in the mirror. I was home alone watching a movie. My mom and dad took the twins out to Chuck E. Cheese for a birthday party, so I was free to order pizza and binge Netflix all on my own. I chose an R-rated movie that my mom probably wouldn't have approved of, but it was already marked as 'watched' in her profile, so I knew she'd never find out I watched it too. It had some super-heavy-duty sex scenes — one where you could even see the guy's naked butt full-on. But I kind of liked it. It got me feeling all hot and tickly, and as the actors were flicking their tongues in and out of each other's mouths, I had an undeniable urge to feel what it would be like to have someone else's lips on my lips, someone else's tongue touching my tongue. Would I even know what to do?

I went to my bathroom and closed the door. I stretched across the sink and in toward the mirror. Once I was in position, I leaned in toward myself and closed my eyes. I willed myself to imagine that it was Drake or Shawn Mendez across from me, aching to kiss me back. Funny enough, the face that came into my mind was Jared from the frozen yogurt shop. It surprised me, I have to admit, because I hadn't really thought of him since the day he'd walked me home. Or maybe I just didn't want to acknowledge that I'd thought of him. Because really, I'd never thought of anyone in that way, ever.

I felt my lips touch the cool of the mirror, and I parted them just enough so that my tongue could slip out and flick the glass. I imagined that Jared's hands were gently cupping my face and tickling the back of my neck. My eyes blinked open at the unexpected cool glossiness of the mirror, and through the foggy patch my breath made, I could make out the crusty acne clusters on my dark skin and my out-of-control hair crunched into the mirror. I pulled back immediately, embarrassed and ashamed. The fog on the glass cleared and I was left looking at my own reflection. No one would ever want to kiss that—not even Jared.

So now I stand here transfixed beside the school bathroom, imagining two warm bodies discovering each other beyond that door, when Sean Fedun's unmistakable gravelly voice pulls me out of my daydream.

"Come on. Let's try something new, Kayla," I hear him plead.

"No, we've been gone for too long. Someone is going to come looking for us. We better go."

"Come on. Let's stay for just a bit."

"No, Sean, not at school. Okay? I don't want to get in trouble. As it is, we reek, and we're going to have a tough time explaining this."

"Just try putting your hand here for a bit. Yeah, that feels so good. Don't you like making me feel good? Now just kneel down. Don't worry. I'll show you what to do."

I can't tell what's happening in the stall but there seems to be a bit of a scuffle, judging by the movement of their sneakers and Kayla's constant, yet timid 'no's'. In an instant, I see her knees thunk down to the floor in front of Sean and I hear the unzip of a zipper.

I don't know what to do. Part of me wants to go grab a teacher, but I'm not quite that brave. And how would I even explain this to a teacher? Kayla and Sean hate me enough that I don't need a new target on my back by getting them in trouble. I'm not sure I have enough guts to step in and stop it either. I mean, who am I to do that anyway? Maybe they're having a good time and they'll be super-pissed if I interrupt? But a little voice in my head knows this isn't right.

Emboldened with newfound courage, I stomp loudly into the bathroom. I go into one of the empty stalls and slam the door harshly, so it's obvious they aren't alone in the bathroom anymore. I go on to blow my nose and flush the toilet — anything to announce my presence. I hear Kayla hop onto her feet and Sean sigh in aggravation. From the safety of my bathroom stall, I hear the zip of his jeans once again, the door to their bathroom stall violently bangs open and heavy footsteps sulk off down the hall.

I wait in the stall a few more moments until I feel I am alone once again.

But when I slowly push the door of the stall open, I see Kayla standing at the sink, trying in vain to use a scratchy paper towel to wipe away the mascara that has smeared down her cheeks. I say nothing and neither does she. I try to make eye contact with her in the mirror, but she avoids my gaze at all costs. It seems that even now nothing has changed. I am simply invisible.

* * * *

By the time I make it back to class, the bell has already rung. I'm aware that I'm probably going to have to field questions from Ms. Kelly about where I've been for the last twenty minutes, but since 'the incident', all the teachers in the school have given me a little more leeway about things.

I wait for the other kids to file out before I try to sneak in to grab my stuff. But when I get to my desk, it's empty and I'm left feeling a bit panicked. My backpack has my binder, a couple of textbooks and the three most recent library books that I've taken out. I have a history test tomorrow, and this is not the time for me to lose all my stuff.

I'm about to walk up to Ms. Kelly to see if she has taken my things when I feel a hand touch me on the shoulder.

"Here, Jodie. I grabbed your stuff for you. Is everything okay? You were gone for a long time."

It's Rebecca Sherman speaking to me, for the second time today. And she's holding my backpack in her free arm. She reaches out to pass it to me and also slides a sheet of paper from her own binder.

"Ms. Kelly also gave us the next novel study assignment. Looks like we're doing *Artemis Fowl*, which isn't really my thing, but it shouldn't be too difficult. She wants us to read the first two Chapters for tomorrow."

"Uh, wow, thanks for doing that. I wasn't super-keen on sneaking back into class and having to have a one-on-one with Ms. Kelly. You know how she gets when she starts lecturing about missing class. I'd be stuck there for an extra half an hour."

Rebecca smiles politely and the conversation fades into silence. I desperately want to think of something to say so she'll stay and chat for a while longer. I'm about to ask if she wants to go grab a snack after school and we can start the book together. I open my mouth and will the words to tumble out, but they're stuck at the back of my throat like scared animals in a cage. I finally take a deep breath and am about to jump off the cliff when Kayla bursts into the conversation.

"OMG, Rebecca, I've been looking everywhere for you! Sean and I ditched LA so we could vape in the bathroom and now I am feeling soooo great. And I seriously have the munchies. Come on. Let's go grab a bite on our way home!"

Kayla avoids my gaze the entire time she speaks, and it's not until she's turned Rebecca around that she allows our eyes to meet. The look she gives me simply reconfirms what I already know. What I saw didn't happen and I need to go back to my own territory.

Chapter Thirteen

Sometimes, on my way home from school, I like to treat myself. It's my way of ending the day on a good note, even if it was a shitty day. My mom hates that I do this and is always trying to convince me to *'save my money'* and *'eat a healthy snack'* at home. Screw that. I earn a bit of money babysitting Anna and Amy on the weekends, and I deserve to spend it however I like.

On Wednesdays I typically walk home from school, as my mom doesn't work from home on Wednesdays and usually gets home late. I alternate between stopping by the fancy cupcake store or just grabbing a slushie and a chocolate bar from the gas station. I guess I should be saving my money to buy something more exciting than a Twix bar several days a week. I mean, other kids my age are already saving up to buy a car. But there's nothing I really need or want. I'm not into clothes or makeup, and it's not like I typically need money to go out on the weekend.

Today it's incredibly hot and I'm almost wishing my mom had picked me up instead. I feel sweat slipping between my thighs as I walk, and I'm pretty sure my bra is soaked through. The burst of sunlight through my bedroom window must have made me feel a bit daring this morning, because I put on a bright flowery dress with a pair of flip-flops instead of my usual boring attire. My mom bought me this dress when we had to go to a cousin's baptism last summer, as she was appalled that I was planning on attending it in leggings and a T-shirt. I fought her tooth and nail on the issue, but she wouldn't budge, even threatening to take my library card away if I didn't pick an outfit. So, I reluctantly trudged through the mall with her for an hour and a half, disappointment growing at each store we went to with the lack of choices available for a *'girl my size'*. Those are Mom's words, not mine. That's why I stick to leggings and a T-shirt. They're never too short, never too tight, and I always blend with a crowd.

I was almost winning the battle against my mom, right up until the point that we turned to walk back down the last corridor in the mall. And there was *Long Tall Sally*. The one store I knew would have clothes that fit me in the physical sense, but I knew they wouldn't fit *me*. They're all made for middle-aged moms who want to try to look like their 'pre-baby' days.

So, I was super-surprised when my mom passed me this flowery sundress over the top of the change room door, and I wasn't immediately repulsed. The pale greens and blues really complemented my dark skin, and when I put it on, the waistline hugged just a bit at that spot where your belly meets your ribs. It's my most narrow part, so it made me somehow look smaller than I am, and the bias-cut of the skirt camouflaged my big rear-end. It had a lower-cut top than I've ever worn in my life, but I found that I kind of liked how it accentuated the smooth, coffee-colored curves of my chest. So, even though it was a dress, and I vowed I would *never* wear a dress, I willingly brought it home.

Granted, it has sat in my closet until today, and I don't know what made me pick it to wear this morning. I just felt like looking pretty-*ish*, I guess.

Pretty-*ish* is unfortunately *not* what I'm feeling as I trudge home after school in this heat. I'm about to call off the whole after-school-treat tradition altogether, when I remember the frozen yogurt place in the strip mall with the library.

The one where *Hi, I'm Jared* works.

On Wednesday afternoons.

I literally can't get there soon enough and I'm huffing and puffing by the time I pull open the double doors to the gloriously air-conditioned room.

I am half terrified and half elated when I catch a glimpse of him behind the counter, his back to me as he's re-stacking the waffle cones. I'm suddenly panicked about what to do now.

Call over to him from across the store like we're best friends?

Ignore him altogether and pretend to forget that he works here?

Turn the other way because I've just realized how absolutely insane this idea was in the first place?

I am caught between choosing number two and number three when I hear my name called from the far end of the store. I glance over at the tables to see where the voice is coming from and see Bethany and Karen waving me over.

I completely forgot that it's Wednesday, and they have their weekly Wednesday frozen yogurt date. I catch myself smiling as I remember Bethany's voice verbatim, *'Chocolate fudge with sprinkles in a cup, not a cone. Never a cone.'*

I figure that they have just given me a choice of a number four — head directly to their table and avoid placing an order at the counter altogether.

Easy decision.

As I approach them, I offer a quiet hello, but before I even finish saying the word, Bethany jumps up and starts flapping her hands.

"That's Jodie McGavin. She likes frozen yogurt, Karen. Jodie McGavin likes frozen yogurt this Wednesday!"

She's so excited that the other customers start to look around, wondering what's going on. I find it hilarious that they're looking around to see someone important or famous, and literally, she's just talking about *me*.

With her loud outburst, I know that Jared has probably heard as well, but I resist every urge to look over in his direction to see. Instead, I turn so my back is facing the counter, and I slide in across from them in the booth.

"Hi, Bethany. Hi, Karen. I forgot you guys were usually here on Wednesdays. I just came by quickly to grab a cone. God, it's so hot today…" *Why do I always resort to talking about the weather? It's no wonder no one ever wants to speak to me.*

"Jodie McGavin, you're getting a *cone*? I don't like cones. Always a cup. Only a cup. And chocolate fudge. Are you getting chocolate fudge?"

"Remember, Bethany, that we've talked about how everyone can have different tastes and that's okay.

Jodie may not like chocolate fudge, but we're not going to get upset about it. You can just enjoy eating *your* chocolate fudge."

I can tell by the restlessness of her fingers and the speed of her rocking that Bethany is starting to get agitated. It's like Karen senses her anxiety and simply holds Bethany's hands in her own, rubbing the backs of them with repetitive circles.

"Sorry. I didn't mean to upset her. I'll just get going."

"No, wait. Stay with us. This is exactly the kind of situation we've been working on with Bethany. She can be a bit rigid, and the only way for her to get out of these perseverative thoughts is to be pushed a bit. She really likes being around you, so I think this is good for her. Honestly, just stay."

As I sit awkwardly in the booth across from Bethany, I curse the fact that I'm in a dress. My sweaty legs are already sticking so badly to the cheap nylon. I feel a rip under my right thigh, and it scratches me every time I shift a little, so I attempt to sit perfectly still, with sweat now pooling between my thighs.

"Is it a special occasion today? You look really pretty in that dress," Karen comments, after a moment or two go by without conversation.

I'm not about to go on about the fact that this is my only dress and how it does make me feel sort of pretty, so I just shake my head no and look down at my lap.

"You know, I get it, Jodie. I get you. God, I *was* you." Karen stares directly at me, her gorgeous brown eyes like laser beams trying to bore into me.

"You feel like you don't belong, that you don't fit in, right? You like spending time alone because it feels — I don't know — safer. Am I right? And at the end of the day, you lie in bed and cry because you're so *lonely*. You chastise yourself for not reaching out to anyone, because really, it's you who has set up these walls, and you vow that the next day you're going to be just a little bit braver, that you're not going to care so much. But then the next day comes and you don your cloak of invisibility again and it's like Groundhog Day over and over."

Karen blurts all this out at once, without even really taking a breath. I wasn't prepared for such a transparent glimpse into my soul, so I'm not even sure how to respond. I mean, she pretty much just hit me bang on, but it's not like I'm going to admit that. And where does she get all this anyway?

"Jodie, I was fifteen once too, remember? And God, was I ever awkward. You should have seen me. I was scrawny as hell. I don't think I made it past a hundred pounds until I was in my twenties. I remember the boys always making fun of my flat chest, calling me a surfboard and everything. And I had weird interests. I was into fairies and wizards and stuff. That wasn't cool back then. Trust me. When I was sixteen, I actually thought I was some kind of sorceress you know, like a witch, I guess? It's super-embarrassing to say now, but I even tried making up potions to get the other kids to like me a little more. This boy — Robbie Jordan, to be specific... Well, I can tell you that backfired big-time. Once the other kids found out what I was into, everyone not only thought I was weird, but I think they were actually scared of me. God, high school was just awful!

"But you know, I was just a kid trying to figure things out, the same as everyone else. It didn't help that I was the only half-Columbian, half-Filipino kid in the school — in the world, probably. I just couldn't figure out how and where I fit in."

Karen goes on to tell me about how she was one of the only ethnic minorities in her entire school and how she was the only person she knew that was mixed race. Her parents met each other in their English language learning class when they first moved to Phoenix. Her dad didn't know a word of Spanish, her mom had no clue how to speak Filipino and they were both just beginning to learn English. But I guess they found a way to fall in love, eventually get married then have Karen. She tells me how the other kids always turned their noses up at her at lunchtime, when she'd have *empanadas* or *pancit* in her Thermos instead of a bologna sandwich. She never really had birthday parties as they lived in a small one-bedroom apartment, so there wasn't much room. So, she spent a lot of her childhood immersed in books, not unlike me. She got wrapped up into different legends and mythologies and felt most comfortable imagining herself in a different world from the current one.

"Then, one summer as a teenager, I worked at a camp for special-needs kids. For the first time in my life, I felt like no one there cared about my ethnic background, how I looked or whether I was into fairies or werewolves or anything. The kids and counselors alike showed interest in *me*, and for once I felt confident enough to share my passions with them. That's when I met an eight-year-old Bethany. I was automatically attracted to Bethany's honest and 'no bullshit' approach to life. Even as a little kid, Bethany did what she wanted, said what she felt and didn't care what other people thought of her." Karen chuckles softly to herself as she recalls Bethany's feisty personality and I can't help but agree with her.

These personal revelations about Karen and her difficulties when growing up make me view her through a completely different lens. I have a tough time looking at this beautiful, self-assured twenty-six-year-old in front of me and thinking of her as an awkward teenager.

"Trust me, Jodie. High school kind of sucks for everyone, even the Kayla Suttons of the world. And you never really know what other people are going through, because every kid in high school locks their secrets up so no one will ever see them."

I think back to Kayla and Sean in the bathroom and the look of fear and sadness in her eyes afterward. Maybe there is something to what Karen is saying.

"My advice to you is to stick with the people who make you feel good being you. Soon enough, you'll get older — and braver — and you'll feel a whole lot freer to express who you are. And from what I see, you're a pretty awesome chick."

As if right on cue, I feel a tap on my shoulder and see Jared standing beside our table, awkwardly shuffling from one foot to the other.

"Hey, Jodie. How's it going? I wasn't sure if it was you at first when you walked in, but then I heard your friends announce your name, so I knew it had to be. You look so different today. You're wearing a dress. That dress... Well, it looks really pretty on you." As he says this, I notice his eyes flick for a second down to the expanse of smooth cleavage on display from his vantage point standing above me. I know I should feel somewhat insulted by his gaze, but instead I'm feeling a little appreciative. Confident, even.

"Hey, Jared. Great to see you. Um, these are my friends Bethany and Karen. Guys, this is Jared." My face feels about a dozen degrees warmer as I do these introductions and I know Karen is suppressing a smirk the entire time. I'm just grateful that Bethany can't see my face, as she would surely comment on its suddenly changing color.

"Can I get you the regular, Jodie? Or are you going to be adventurous today?" He casually punches me on the shoulder as if we're best buddies and I like it. I really like it. I'm not sure I've ever realized how exciting it can feel for someone to gently punch you on the shoulder.

I guess it matters who the *someone* is.

I also didn't ever realize how cute anyone could be wearing a teal-blue apron, a hair net with a ball cap and a set of disposable plastic gloves. The surprises today are endless.

"Actually, I am feeling a bit daring today, so bring me the regular on a cone, but with caramel drizzle on top as well." I do my best to give him a dazzling smile, capturing my inner Karen. And I'm surprised that it makes me feel, well…a bit dazzling. I think I'm flirting for real this time!

A few minutes later, Jared arrives back at our table with my cone, complete with the caramel drizzle on top and with an extra little bowl of gummy bears on the side.

"I brought you guys some extra gummy bears to snack on. You know, in case you want a little more." He then stands awkwardly for a moment, pretending to wipe his hands on his apron.

"So, I guess I should get back to work." He pauses once more momentarily then turns to me. "Jodie, are you going to be at the library any time later this week? I could maybe pop by to say hi or you could come by here during my break. Or whatever... I mean, if you don't have other stuff going on."

My heart feels like it is literally going to burst out of my body but I'm trying my best to stay super-cool. I'm pretty sure my chest is heaving so hard that Jared thinks I'm having a panic attack, but when I speak, I'm able to at least make my voice sound calm and self-assured.

"Yeah, sure. That'd be fun. I have a science quiz coming up later in the week and seeing as you're the 'super-nerd, homeschooled brainiac', I bet you could help me study." I smirk when I say this and look up at him with slightly arched eyebrows. *Score one more flirting point for Jodie McGavin. Where did all of this come from?*

"Sure thing. And you can help me write the latest book report my mom wants me to do on *The Outsiders*. You just finished that one not too long ago, didn't you?"

Somehow, he convinces me that we need to exchange numbers so we can get a hold of each other besides our chance meetings at the frozen yogurt store. I'm left sitting there looking at the one and only contact in my otherwise-unused phone.

"He seems super-cute, Jodie. Well done!" Karen whispers. I'm not sure what I've done well, but I'm proud of myself, nonetheless.

I focus on eating the last of my frozen yogurt for a few moments, thinking about how my entire life has shifted so much in just a few short weeks. A couple of my gummy bears land on the table, and I see Bethany's restless hands find one and roll it between her thumb and forefinger. Karen explains that it's a candy she can eat, and despite several loud announcements that she *'does not like gummy bears'*, Karen convinces her to pop one in her mouth. She chews reluctantly at first then erupts into a burst of giggles seemingly when the taste explodes in her mouth.

"Jodie, did you ever eat a gummy bear? They are so slippery in my mouth, like a slippery strawberry. I want more gummy bears. More slippery, strawberry gummy bears."

"Yeah, I guess sometimes it's surprising how much you like something once you give it a try, Bethany."

We laugh and enjoy spending the next several minutes stuffing our faces with gummy bears, as if discovering the taste of the delicious, slippery candies for the first time.

Chapter Fourteen

When we get up to leave the frozen yogurt restaurant, I find myself gently guiding Bethany out of the bench seat again without really thinking about it. I'm the one sitting right opposite her, so it feels natural for me to link her arm around my elbow and guide her around the cluster of tables and chairs and out into the hot afternoon sunshine. The three of us walk quietly along the sidewalk of the main road, Bethany's cane making the *tick tick* of a metronome in time with our footsteps.

Before I've even thought about where we're going, we end up in front of a cute brick two-story house with a red painted door and a perfectly manicured lawn.

"Well, we're here, at Bethany's house. Why don't you come in for a bit, Jodie? My shift is over, but I'm going to pop in for a minute to chat with Bethany's mom. I'll introduce you. She'll be thrilled that Bethany has brought a friend over."

Reluctantly, I follow Karen up the front walk, Bethany the one guiding me now. Karen lets herself into the house without knocking, and we all spend a few moments in the front room taking off our shoes.

The house is cool, clearly air-conditioned, and I feel a rush of relief after walking in the hot sun. Bethany's mom comes in from the hall when she hears us and immediately goes over to Bethany, grabbing her cane from her and putting it aside. She gives Bethany a huge squeeze, a kiss on the cheek then turns her attention to me.

"Let me guess. You must be Jodie McGavin. Bethany has been speaking so much about you. Karen mentioned that you've been a huge help welcoming Bethany into the new school as well. It's been so great to hear, as sometimes things can be kind of tough with Bethany. Care to stay for supper? It's taco night and everything should be ready in about an hour."

"And that's my cue to leave as well. I'm meeting some friends for dinner tonight and I've got to run home to let my cats out first." Karen grabs her purse and turns to leave.

"Jodie, it was really great chatting today. Have fun hanging with Bethany and we'll see you at school tomorrow, okay?"

Then before I know it, Karen is out of the door, Bethany is standing beside me, fingers flicking furiously in front of her face, and Bethany's mom is standing there with her hands on her hips, an expectant smile on her face.

I'm feeling so incredibly awkward. Up until now things were fine, great even. But I had Karen to chat with, acting as a buffer between Bethany and me. Now

I don't know what to do. I've gotten myself into this weird situation, but I'm not sure how to get out.

I think Mrs. Robertson senses my hesitation because she immediately turns and speaks to Bethany.

"Bethany, sweetie, why don't you take Jodie upstairs to your room and you two can listen to music or something? Alyssa will be home from a friend's in a few minutes, so you have Jodie all to yourself before your sister tries to steal her away. You know how Alyssa likes to capture everyone's attention."

"Yeah, Alyssa is bossy. She's such a bossy girl. She's always in my room touching my stuff. I don't like it when Alyssa touches my stuff." Bethany turns abruptly and, using the handrail for support, walks straight up the staircase to her right. I wait for a moment, then decide she's not going to check whether I'm coming, so I scoot up behind her.

When I get to the landing at the top of the stairs, I pause for a moment to take out my phone. I know my mom will be expecting me home for dinner, so I've got to give her a heads-up. I don't want to tell her exactly where I am, especially after our discussion with Mr. Rutter. I decide simplicity is best and text a quick '*At a friend's for dinner. Be home by eight.*' I'll leave the detailed explanation for later.

Bethany's room is the first door on the left, and I'm taken aback when I first step inside. It is over-the-top girly, like something out of a Barbie dreamhouse. Everything in it is a different shade of pink, and there are ruffles on the pillows, the window seat and the four-poster bed. It literally looks like it was the set used in Katie Perry's *California Gurls* video.

"Wow, you must really like the color pink, Bethany," I say, not hiding my sarcasm.

"Mom likes pink. She says all girls like pink. Pink is pretty for girls," Bethany responds, then sits and rocks on the side of the bed, fingering the ruffle from one of the pillow shams.

I continue making my way around the room, inspecting all the details, when it hits me. *Bethany can't even see any of this.* Pink isn't something that Bethany can see or even imagine. The flowers in the wallpaper go unappreciated every day. The pictures on the wall of ballerinas in various poses and positions are unseen. Who are these things even for, if not for Bethany? It's like Bethany's parents have created a room for a different child — one who can see color, dance in pirouettes around the room and appreciate the beauty of a brushstroke. It makes me feel unbelievably sad for a moment, like this room has been designed based on a dream that will never become a reality. I finally make my way to the bed and sit beside Bethany, who has remained quiet the entire time I've done my snooping.

"So, what do you like to do for fun then, Bethany?" I ask, willing her to respond with something constructive we can do together.

"I like to read, mostly Stephen King. I read all the Stephen King books. Everyone says they're scary, but I don't think they're scary. I like the words he uses. *Wendy, darling. Light of my life... I'm not gonna hurt ya. I'm just going to bash in your brains.*" Her voice changes dramatically to a male voice with a slight Southern drawl, and it takes me a minute to register what she's saying and why. The quote is close to one from Stephen King's *The Shining*. I wouldn't know, except that I'm currently on a Stephen King kick myself and *The Shining* is one of my favorites.

I rack my brain for a minute then remember something of the phrase I'm looking for.

"*Monsters and ghosts are real. They live in us, and sometimes, they win.*" I can't manage the accent quite as well as Bethany, but as soon as I finish my attempt at the quote, she erupts into a fit of giggles and squeals.

"Jodie, that was so good. You are so good at that! Do it again. Again, Jodie!" I come up with as many quotes as I can remember and find myself laughing more freely every time I speak. My accent has taken a dramatic turn and Bethany and I both burst into giggles when it comes out with a Scottish lilt instead of a country drawl. Before I know it, we've been having this ping-pong of back-and-forth impersonations for twenty minutes. Karen was right. Bethany is as well-read as anyone I know, and I find it funny that she enjoys a lot of the same books that I do.

As I look over to her bookshelf filled with braille books, I notice a large stack of blank paper and it gives me an idea.

"Hey, Bethany, do you want to learn some more origami? I could teach you to make more than just a butterfly?"

"I like that butterfly, Jodie McGavin. I would like to make more butterflies. Could you teach me how to make a monarch or a mountain ringlet?"

"Yeah, I could try," I respond. To me a butterfly is a butterfly and I really don't know the difference between any of them, but as I go through the steps of folding with her, I make minor changes, each time making a slightly different shape. She is thrilled and follows along avidly, not getting stuck, even with the tricky parts.

Before we know it, the floor of her room is covered in a smattering of paper butterflies. The door bursts open and a little girl of about five or six bounds in.

"Hey, Beth Beth Bo Beth!" the little girl screeches and runs full tilt toward Bethany before piling on top of her with a giant bear hug. It causes Bethany to fall back awkwardly on the bed. I notice that she doesn't really hug her sister back, but just sort of lets herself be mauled for a minute before returning to a sitting position. The little girl now sits on the edge of the bed between Bethany and me.

"So, you're Jodie?" the little girl asks me quizzically. "Bethy never had a friend over before. What are you guys doing? You have a pretty dress on. Your hair is really poofy. Hey, guys, want to play American Girls?"

Without waiting for a single response, she bounds into a room down the hall and comes back with two American Girl dolls and an armful of outfits.

"Sorry... I don't have any American Girls with black skin, so you'll just have to be her." She thrusts a doll with long black hair and piercing blue eyes into my arms. "I get to be Charlotte cuz she's my favorite one."

"What about Bethany? Do you have one for her?" I pipe up.

"No, Bethany can't really play that good. She doesn't know how to pretend stuff. Oh, but she's really good at doing their hair and dressing them. Show her how you can do the braids, Bethy. Show her!"

Alyssa places the doll in Bethany's lap, and as her hands touch the doll's hair, her fingers begin to move at a lightning-fast pace. She grabs section after section of hair, her fingers like nimble knitting needles working on a project. I am floored by the skill and speed with which she works, and I have to keep reminding myself that she can't even see what she's doing.

"Wow, Bethany, you are incredible at that. How did you learn to braid so quickly?"

"Mom taught her on my hair one day when we were waiting at a doctor's appointment. Bethany used to *really* like pulling hair and she would sometimes pull my hair super-hard when I was little. Mom used to get mad at her and I would cry and cry. But Mom says Bethy wasn't trying to be mean. She just likes how my hair feels. I have super-soft hair. Here, feel!" She tilts her head over to me so I can run my fingers through her silky strands.

"Bethy likes to do stuff with her hands so her doctor told Mom, *'Teach her to do something else instead of pulling hair.'* So, Mom taught her how to braid. Now, if she knows your hair is down, she'll just do one hundred braids all over your head. Sometimes it looks funny, but at least it doesn't hurt."

By this time, Alyssa's doll's head is almost full of teeny braids sticking up all over. As she waits for Bethany to finish, I notice that Alyssa is busy tracing hearts onto the side of Bethany's leg. The two of them seem so — I don't know — at ease with each other. Most of the time when Anna or Amy come into my room, I'm quick to boot them out. I don't know the last time I've played American Girls with either one of them. And we definitely don't sit and snuggle or do each other's hair. *Maybe I should try teaching them to braid one day?*

I'm lost in thought when I hear Alyssa start chirping again.

"How 'bout you let Bethy do your hair, Jodie? It'll look really pretty when it's done. And maybe it won't be so...*bushy* after."

Alyssa stands up from where she's been seated between Bethany's legs and pulls me down to that spot instead. She grabs Bethany's hands and guides them over to my head.

I feel her fingers eagerly explore my head. At first, she just grabs handfuls of hair, wrapping the strands in and around her fingers then running her fingers from the scalp to the ends. Every time she does this, I brace a little, ready for her to start yanking chunks out. But it never gets to this point. She always pulls a little then stops abruptly, like she remembers what she's allowed to do. At one point her fingers still for a moment, and I'm pretty sure she is burying her face into the back of my head. I'm glad I had a shower yesterday, because this would be way more embarrassing if my hair was greasy.

"Mmm-m, Jodie McGavin, your hair smells just like coconut." Bethany takes a deep breath in at the back of my hair. She just stays like that with her fingers scrunching and twirling around my hair and her face buried inside. It feels extremely intimate and pretty weird, to tell the truth. But, at the same time, I kind of like it. Sort of the same feeling as when you're little and your mom gives you back tickles before you fall asleep.

"Bethy, you're being kinda weird. I know Jodie's hair feels cool, but just show her how you can *braid!*" Alyssa insists, displaying the impatience of a six-year-old.

"I like to braid. I can braid Jodie McGavin's hair. Jodie McGavin has coconut hair. And it feels so squishy. Not slippery like Alyssa's hair. Or my hair. We have slippery hair. Jodie, you have squishy, smooshy, tickly hair. It smells like coconut."

With that, I feel her fingers start working. They grab tiny pieces of hair and weave in and out of each other until a braid is complete and she moves on to another spot. I forgot how satisfying it is for someone to just play with my hair. I find myself relaxing into the sensation and close my eyes. I hear Bethany start to hum a song and it only takes me a moment to recognize it as a jazz piece by Dave Brubeck. I'm blown away, as there aren't many fifteen-year-olds into jazz.

"*Take Five* by Dave Brubeck, right? I love that piece," I tell her.

Bethany doesn't answer as she seems lost in her own world, so I don't ask again. I just join her in humming and continue while she finishes up with my hair.

A few minutes later, her fingers come to an abrupt halt and she drops her hands at her side.

"There's no more hair left," she says simply, and she just sits there. I take this as my cue to get up. I look around for a mirror so I can see the finished product, but then I remember. *Why would Bethany have a mirror in her room, when she can't ever see herself?* I wonder what it would be like not to see yourself. I think it would be awesome not to see myself every day, not to have to look in the mirror and deal with what's looking back at me. Although, it's not like everybody else would be blind too. They would still see how ugly I am. I just wouldn't see it for myself. Then I imagine how hard it would be to get ready for the day. *How would you know if you have toothpaste on your face? How would you know whether you have a huge zit on your chin? How would you know anything?*

I glance back at Bethany sitting on the bed and I'm struck by how *pretty* she is. I mean, she's not like a sprite or anything, but all things considered, she's always so well put together. Her hair is always neatly pulled back into a ponytail. Her clothes always look decent. You can tell her mom probably shops for her because she's usually wearing button-down shirts and jeans, but still. Everything for her has gotta be so much work. And I bet she needs to rely on other people to help her with just about *everything*. I start to wonder about when she goes to the bathroom. *Does she do everything herself? What about when she gets her period? How would she even know she has her period without being able to see anything?* I think back to 'the incident' and realize that if it were Bethany there, not me, she wouldn't even have *realized* anything embarrassing had happened. She would have heard the whispers maybe, but she wouldn't have been able to see the teasing looks on everyone's eyes or the way people would have inched just a little farther from her when she sat down.

I think the not-knowing would be worse. Way worse.

It's all getting a bit much for me, and suddenly, the problems I have seem pretty trivial. So what if I don't wear the coolest clothes? Why does that even matter? And big deal if I'm a little bigger than everyone else. Why should they care?

I'm in the middle of my little confidence pep-talk when I flick the light on in the bathroom across the hall from Bethany's room. I am stunned at what I see in the reflection looking back at me in the mirror.

The person in the mirror has a thousand tiny braids popping out in all directions, like a million little dreads. With my hair off my face, my deep brown eyes look a little brighter and a little bigger. My zits are still there, sure. And I still have the slight double-chin, the result of one too many Oreo-hoarding parties in my room. But

I'm struck by how much the girl looking back at me reminds me of my six-year-old self, of when my mom used to take me to get my hair done in tiny braids every three weeks, of back tickles and nighttime snuggles. I tear up remembering those days and desperately want them back again.

My quiet moment is disrupted by Bethany's mom calling us down for dinner. I hear Alyssa race down the stairs and, out of the corner of my eye, I see Bethany walk out of her room, fingers once again flicking each other in front of her face. She doesn't stop to check on me or see if I'm coming. I guess she knows I can just figure things out for myself. And I do. I always do.

* * * *

After dinner, I thank Mrs. Robertson and start to say my goodbyes. She responds with another giant bear hug, which takes me by surprise.

"Well, we loved having you over, Jodie. Please feel that you are welcome here anytime. I know Bethany really enjoyed having you."

"Jodie McGavin has coconut hair. It doesn't feel bushy anymore. Mom, her hair doesn't feel bushy. It smells like coconut. And it's not so bushy." Jodie keeps rambling on as I get my shoes on. She doesn't say goodbye to me or even really acknowledge that I'm leaving. But I can tell it bothers her because her hands start waving beside her face instead of just flicking softly in front of her. As I walk down the front steps, I hear her mom trying to soothe her.

"Honey, it's okay. Jodie has to head back to her own house now, but I'm sure she'll be back. You'll see her again soon." And instead of being weirded out by the comment, it makes me feel content to know I have a place here anytime I want.

I walk the twenty minutes or so back home. When I get to the front walk, I remember that I have the crazy braids in my hair and for a moment I debate taking them out. But I decide they give me a bohemian look that kind of reminds me of Miss Karen, so I choose to keep them. After all, my mom is always after me to do something with my hair.

I plan to go straight upstairs to my room to continue building Harry Potter World, but Amy and Anna catch me as I walk in the front door.

"Whoa, Jodie, what happened to your hair?" Amy blurts out as she walks into the front foyer.

After hearing that comment, Mom strolls in from the kitchen.

When she sees me, she stops dead and she just keeps looking at me up and down. I'm ready for her to make some sort of judgy comment or tell me to go take a shower and take out my ridiculous braids. But instead, she steps in close to me and reaches up with one hand.

"Wow, Jodie, you just look so, so different. Lovely really. Your hair… And your dress… What's the special occasion today?"

I look down, completely forgetting that I even chose to wear this flowery dress today. Now I understand why my mom is so shocked. I definitely don't look like the regular Jodie McGavin who lives in this house.

"How did you even get it done like that? It reminds me of when I used to take you to the salon when you were little. Remember that?" Mom says softly while inspecting each strand.

"Yeah, it actually looks pretty cool," Amy pipes in. "Kind of like an alien from another planet mixed with

Princess Rapunzel. Can I feel it?" And she reaches over to touch the braids too.

"Uh, sure… It's just my regular hair. I just put it in braids today instead. Well, actually Bethany put it in braids. I kind of, um…hung out with her today. At her place. Except the braids are starting to come out. I didn't secure the ends very well." I'm not sure how Mom is going to react to the realization that I've been hanging out with the 'special-needs kid', and I cringe to hear her response.

"Wow, Bethany did that? Well, isn't that impressive? Did you have a good time at her place?" she questions cautiously.

"Yeah, actually I did," I find myself saying. And I'm even more surprised to find that it's the truth.

"Well, I'm really glad you've found someone that you like hanging out with, sweetheart. Good for you." And I'm surprised to find there's honesty in Mom's voice too. I feel relieved and elated at the same time.

"Ok, come here, honey. I can help you with the braids. I think I've got those clear, tiny elastics around that we used to use." My mom starts rustling through our junk drawer in the kitchen and pulls out a plastic baggie full of elastics. "Come and sit on the couch, Jodie, and I'll fix them."

She sits on the couch and motions for me to sit between her legs, like I did with Bethany. Then she proceeds to fix the braids that were coming undone and secures them with the tiny elastics. It feels so good to be close to Mom again, have her taking care of me. I take a couple of deep breaths so I won't start crying. When Mom finishes, she reaches both arms around my shoulders and gives me a long squeeze.

"You know… You're so grown up and so independent that sometimes I forget to tell you just how much I love you."

The giant lump in my throat prevents me from saying anything back, but I think she knows. Maybe moms always know.

Chapter Fifteen

Walking into school today, I'm not feeling quite as confident about my new hair as I did last night. I pulled the braids up and into a sort of bun on the top of my head, as it's as sweltering today as it was yesterday. But when I looked in the mirror before I left home, I felt like my face was so, well...*visible*, and I'm not sure how I feel about that. I've always imagined my hair as a protective shield, and not having it hang around my shoulders and face makes me almost feel naked.

I also decided to skip the leggings and sweatshirt once more, and I put on a pair of shorts and a T-shirt instead. I haven't worn shorts in a long time, as I've always been so self-conscious about my legs. But I remembered how uncomfortable I felt yesterday in the sweltering heat.

So, as I walk up the front steps of the school, I feel really exposed. I keep my head down so as not to make eye contact with anyone, and I head straight to my locker.

As I'm getting my books out, I hear a cluster of girls whispering behind me.

"What's with Jodie McGavin's hair? Is she trying to be Medusa or something? That is so hideous. And it just makes her look even fatter. OMG, I feel like I'm going to throw up just looking at her." I can tell it's Kayla's voice without even turning around. I don't know what's up with her. Before our 'play date', she was fine. She never paid me attention. I wasn't even on her radar. And since then, it's like she's been out to get me. I don't know what I've done to deserve this. Is she upset that our parents tried to suggest we become friends? Is she embarrassed that I caught her and Sean in the bathroom? I'm gathering the confidence to finally turn around and confront her when Rebecca's voice cuts Kayla's off.

"Kayla, what's your problem with her? She's never done anything to you. Just leave her alone, okay?"

I'm so taken aback by the thought that Rebecca Sherman is actually standing up for me against Kayla Sutton that I just freeze there, facing my locker.

"What's with you lately, Rebecca? Is she your new best friend or something? Zoe said you were, like, sitting next to her in LA class last week, too. Seriously? If that's who you want to hang with, have at 'er. Zoe and I will be over here with the boys."

Out of the corner of my eye, I see Kayla toss back her long blonde hair and stomp off, arm-in-arm with Zoe. And, for a moment, Rebecca doesn't follow. I'm assuming she's still behind me because I haven't heard her move, but I don't want to turn around to see. I hear her take a deep breath and take a step toward me, but then Miss Karen's voice cuts through the quiet hallway.

"Hey, Jodie! I *love* the hair! Bethany told me this morning that she braided your hair and I couldn't figure out what she was talking about. Now I totally get it. It looks awesome!"

"Jodie has coconut hair," Bethany announces, and, without asking for permission, reaches both of her arms out in front of her, searching for my hair. When she feels that it's pulled back in a bun, she gets upset and starts wrenching the braids out. She doesn't give any thought to the fact that it feels like my hair is being ripped from my skull, and she attempts to pile a mound of my braids into her clasped hands while smooshing her face into them, taking giant breaths of air.

It all happens so fast that Karen doesn't have time to react, but now she is trying to gently unclench Bethany's fingers from my scalp.

I'm locked into position by her grasp, and my head is turned up and back at a funny angle. There's a burning sensation shooting through my head and down my neck, until Karen manages to loosen Bethany's hold and get her to take a step away from me. As she does, I notice that Rebecca is no longer standing behind me in the hallway but is awkwardly standing on the cusp of a circle down the hall made up of Kayla, Zoe, Sean and another boy. Karen turns her attention to me.

"Sorry, Jodie. I guess Bethany got a little excited about touching your hair today. I should have been on her quicker than that."

I mumble "No big deal," and begin piling my hair back on the top of my head. As I do so, I again see Kayla's group at the far side of the hall. They are whispering to each other and keep looking over my way. I'm getting really tired of having to put up with the taunting, and I'm eager to just get to class. I abruptly slam my locker shut then turn to leave. But blocking my path is Sean Fedun, now standing directly in front of me, with his posse forming a semicircle behind him.

I glance to the right and see that Karen has pulled Bethany off to the side and is doing her best to calm her after the hair-pulling incident that just occurred. She's not even cognizant that Sean's group has clustered around me.

"Hey, Jodie, nice braids," he starts. "You trying to look pretty for anyone in particular today? I heard Ms. Flanagan is newly single. Maybe she'll dig your new look?" The rest of the group giggle, but I notice that Rebecca has distanced herself noticeably.

"Hey, I have something I want you to take a look at." He quickly whips out a small mirror, like the kind you'd have up in your locker. He huffs onto it with his breath, making it go all foggy. I'm really confused as to what he's trying to show me, but I just stand like a dumbass, as there's not much else for me to do.

He finally turns the mirror around so that it faces me and announces, "Look, Jodie... *Gorillas in the Mist*! You could be the star in the new remake!" Everyone starts laughing, especially Kayla. I notice Sean reach out to grab her around the waist and pull her to him as he high-fives one of the other boys. I look straight ahead, trying not to react, but as the fogginess of the mirror fades, I can make out more and more of the features of my face. My lips are in a tight grimace, and my eyes are cold and dark. I am so done with this, so tired of being tired. I don't even feel the usual lump forming in the back of my throat. I just feel blind fury, as if a hot, molten fireball has formed in the pit of my stomach and the rage within me is willing to spew it out.

"Screw you, Sean Fedun, you self-obsessed, egotistical jerk!"

I have *never* retaliated against Sean Fedun — against anyone, really. I haven't ever really spoken to any of these kids. For a moment, I'm not even sure the words came from my mouth. But the fireball in the pit of my stomach has shrunk a bunch, so I know it must have been me.

For a split second it's quiet, then a shrill voice from across the hall slices the air.

"Screw you, Sean Fedun. Screw you, Sean Fedun. Egotistical jerk. Self-obsessed, egotistical jerk!" The pitch and intonation are a perfect match to my own voice, and I know immediately it's Bethany, repeating my words verbatim. Her echolalia causes her to keep repeating the phrase, over and over, and something miraculous happens.

The laughter turns so that it is now directed at *Sean Fedun*.

His so-called buddies double over in hysterics every time Bethany repeats the phrase. They start chanting it as well, fist-pumping each other and knocking Sean in the shoulder every so often, as if trying to get him to see the humor in the situation. Kayla joins in with the crowd in a sing-song voice, thinking that she's just playing the game and that no harm is really being done.

But when Sean hears her voice join in, his face turns bright red and his eyes glaze over. He roughly shoves her away from him, hard enough that it causes her to stumble backward. She immediately stops chanting and rubs her shoulder where he pushed her. He stomps off alone down the hallway and eventually all the other kids start to disperse to go to class.

Karen has quieted Bethany down so that her chants are simply whispers. I am suddenly aware that she has allowed the incident to carry on, despite being able to stop it long ago. As a staff member, it was probably her obligation to stop it quickly.

"Jodie, are you coming to class?" Karen beckons me.

Before I turn to leave with her and Bethany, I look up to see Rebecca's eyes lock with mine. She gives me the tiniest knowing smirk and an almost-imperceptible nod. And I have to say, I'm feeling pretty good. I continue walking to class alongside Bethany and Karen with the rare realization that my day might be turning right around.

Chapter Sixteen

As it turns out, Bethany and I have gotten into a bit of a routine over the last couple of weeks. And sometimes, I'm surprised by just how much I like hanging out with her. We usually go to her place on Wednesdays, right after we hit the frozen yogurt store. Jared usually waits to take his break until we're there, then sits with us for a half-hour. I don't know if it's because he has a brother with special needs, but he's able to act so normal with Bethany, like she's just a regular person. Which I know she is, but sometimes it feels like most of the world doesn't see that. I'm the first to admit that I didn't before.

Jared has also been meeting me at the library every so often. He says he comes on the pretense that we're studying, but honestly, we've never actually opened a book. I can't even believe I'm saying that. *I'm one of those kids who hangs out at the public library but doesn't even read a book.* I haven't offered for him to come over to my house yet. I'm not ready to navigate that one. How would I introduce him to my mom? As my boyfriend? As just a friend? As the guy who works at the yogurt shop and who doesn't actually go to school? Oh, that would go over so well. No, safer that I keep Jared away from my family, at least for a little while.

A couple of times, Bethany and I have taken Alyssa, Amy and Anna to the park and Jared has tagged along. He's actually super-cute with the girls and we'll all play grounders together for a while. You wouldn't think it, but Bethany is killer at grounders. When you're the one who's it, you have to close your eyes then call 'grounders' when you think someone else is stepping on sand. The rest of us have to just take a wild guess when we call it out, but not Bethany. She's so used to not seeing anything that her ears pick up absolutely everything. There's no way a single one of us can jump down from the monkey bars without her calling us out. And more often than not, she even knows which one of us it is! It feels like creepy voodoo crap, honestly, because sometimes I swear she has magical powers. But I guess that's just Bethany, and she surprises me every day.

Before we leave, we always finish up on the swings. The little girls beg us to push them higher and higher. All three of them fight over which one gets Jared because he can even do under-ducks and they almost fly off. But Bethany loves the swings the most. Something happens to her when she sits and rocks back and forth on those swings. It immediately calms her, stopping all of her finger-flicking and hand-waving. I have to admit I like it too. Sometimes, when we've had a tough day, I'll take Bethany to the park myself. The two of us will just sit in silence alongside each other, swinging back and forth. I think we both love how it feels to have the wind rush through our hair and the way the world is at a standstill while we are the ones moving. I have to admit that she always does this amazing giggle-thing as she swings too high, which always has a way of sweetening my mood.

Today is Saturday, and Bethany's mom called this morning to ask if I wanted to go to the community pool with her. I typically would *never* be caught dead in a swimsuit in front of anyone, really, but her mom was really insistent, so I said I could go. I'm now sitting on my front porch ready to get picked up, and I'm completely regretting my decision.

I hate swimming. I hate being in a swimsuit. What was I thinking?

Mrs. Robertson pulls up a moment later in her Ford Explorer and waves as the car slows to a stop. I climb in and say hi to Bethany, who is sitting in the front seat.

"Jodie, we're going swimming. I love swimming. I go swimming on Saturdays. Swimming on Saturday with Jodie McGavin." She's rocking feverishly back and forth with unbridled enthusiasm.

"You know, Jodie... You certainly made her day when you agreed to come along. I'm sure she's going to have much more fun with you than when I take her." She smiles and winks at me in the rearview mirror.

"Oh, you're not coming along, Mrs. Robertson?" Panic starts to rise in my chest.

"Well, I thought I'd drop the two of you off and go and run a few errands. I'll pick you up at about three p.m. Bethany knows to wear her belted floatie, and the lifeguards there are so great with her, so you really shouldn't have any problems. Don't hesitate to call if you need me to pick you up early."

I'm about to protest or come up with some sort of valid reason why it's not the greatest idea for me to be left alone with Bethany in the pool, but Mrs. Robertson has already parked the car and is walking around to the passenger side to help Bethany climb out.

"Okay, girls, have fun this afternoon!" She kisses Bethany lightly on the cheek and gives me a little wave.

I am trapped.

I take a deep breath and have Bethany grab my elbow, which has become a natural gesture for the both of us. As we get to the front desk, I pay my entrance fee, while the cashier waves Bethany through with her yearly pass. Suddenly we are standing alone in the middle of the tiled change room.

"Jodie, it's time to go in the water." Bethany is already tugging off her T-shirt and attempting to scramble out of her shorts. Her mom had made sure to get her changed into her swimsuit before leaving, so once she tosses her clothes into a locker, she stands there waiting for me to join her.

But I am stuck.

I'm paralyzed with the realization that I haven't gotten my swimsuit on yet, which means I'm going to have to change into it right now, in front of her, exposing everything. *Shit.*

For a minute I toy with the idea of racing to the nearest bathroom stall and quickly changing in there. But I don't trust Bethany to stay put where she is and envision her wandering out onto the pool deck, bailing face-first in the pool. So, my only alternative is that I have to change *in front* of Bethany.

Let me be clear about something. I have never in my entire life gotten naked in front of another human being. Now, granted, I recognize on a surface level that

Bethany is unable to actually see me. I mean, she is blind, after all. But the prospect of stripping down and baring all my bad bits is absolutely overwhelming. I glance around quickly, noticing that the only other people in the change room with us are a couple of old grannies who have just finished their aquacise class and a young mom that is so busy trying to wrangle her toddler into her swimsuit that I don't think she even knows we're in the room.

I take a deep breath and in one fluid movement — well, as fluid as I am ever able to move — I reach down and tug my sweatshirt over my head. It gets caught momentarily on my ponytail, which means my breasts and jiggly middle are exposed for a few seconds more than I expected. But when I glance up to check if Bethany has noticed, she's simply standing in the same spot in front of me, fingers flicking away, waiting for me to lead her through to the exit. Feeling a little braver and a little less self-conscious, I whip down my leggings as well and find myself standing in the middle of the locker room buck naked.

And nothing happens.

No one looks my way. No one teases me or compares me to a narwhal. There are no comments about my breasts being milk jugs or about my bush matching my 'fro hair. It's hard for me to believe, but no one actually cares about how I look, with or without clothes on.

This is the freest I think I have ever felt in my life, and even though she can't see me, I beam the biggest smile at Bethany — or for the first time acknowledge that maybe this is what it's like to have a true friend.

I scramble to pull on my one-piece Speedo, then grab Bethany's arm and pull her forward.

"Hey, Beth, has anyone ever taught you how to do a cannonball?"

After wading in the shallow part of the pool for a while, we decide to go into the dive tank. As Mrs. Robertson promised, Bethany's strict sense of routine ensures that she won't go near the dive tank without a floatation belt. Once we get that strapped on her, she reaches out to feel whether I've got one on too.

"Jodie, you need a floatie. You can't go into the dive tank without a floatie."

"Beth, I'm a pretty good swimmer. I should be okay."

"Jodie, you need a floatie. You can't go into the dive tank without a floatie." Bethany says it over and over like a CD on repeat. I could go and argue with her for another half an hour about this, but if there's one thing about Bethany, it's that she's stubborn. And somehow, she always gets her way.

"Okay, okay. I'll put on a floatie too. See? It's on." I let her feel around my waist until she is satisfied, then we walk to the edge of the dive tank together.

Without thinking, I reach down with my right hand to grab her left. This immediately quiets the flicking for a moment and I take the opportunity to begin counting...

"One, two, three!" With a squeal of delight, I feel the deliciously cold water wrap itself around me. But I never let go of her hand.

Have you ever noticed what happens when you eat a bowl of cereal, and you have two Cheerios left bobbing around in your milk when you're done? No matter where in the bowl they start out, they always end up floating beside each other in the end. I guess that's the best way to describe me and Bethany today.

We just close our eyes and bob around the pool. And unfailingly, we always end up side by side in the end.

Being with Bethany is different from being with other fifteen-year-olds. I never have to feel awkward in conversations, because there's no pressure to talk. Bethany basically speaks her mind all the time with no filter, but she never expects — or really cares — whether I respond. And when I talk to her, she has absolutely no judgment toward me. Sometimes I wonder whether she's even heard what I've said, but then at some point later in the day, she'll recall a sentence or unique word I used and repeat it over and over again. So, I guess she really is listening. She still repeats my comment to Sean Fedun, and it makes me laugh every…single…time.

But mostly when we're together, we just sit quietly and do our own thing, although I guess we kind of do them together. It reminds me of the days when Mom, Dad and I would entangle ourselves on the couch Saturday mornings, immersed in the different worlds of our own books. I find the same comfort being with Bethany. It just feels — I don't know — like *home*.

Chapter Seventeen

I've brought Bethany back to my house today after school. She's really into Stephen King's *It* so I was going to let her just listen to the audiobook while I try to finish up my Harry Potter World display. It's turning out amazing, and I don't even feel embarrassed saying that. I've dedicated an entire shelf to the creation and even moved all my elephants so now they have to share the shelf with the insects. It doesn't seem so important that they don't have their own space anymore.

I'm sitting cross-legged on the floor, folding one of the last turrets for Hogwarts. I'm having such a tough time getting the peak to stand straight up at the exact angle I want, so I have to keep throwing papers aside to start again. At some point, Bethany quietly slinks to the floor beside me. She doesn't say anything but just reaches over to grab the papers I'm folding, her hands hungry rodents grasping at anything she can touch. She does this when she wants to join in with whatever I'm doing. I've gotten used to it as her way of asking. I slide a paper over to her then we start the turret from the beginning. I have to explicitly enunciate and explain each step, occasionally reaching over and helping to guide her hands. It always amazes me how quickly she catches on when I show her, considering she can't see what she's doing.

Over the last several weeks I've taught her the code names for certain basic origami moves, which makes teaching her way easier. So instead of telling her to *fold the right corner down and to the left at a ninety-degree angle*, I can usually just say, *do a mountain fold, then a petal fold, then an inside-out-reverse fold.* We continue like this for several minutes working on various projects, then I come up with the most amazing idea.

"Hey, Bethany, wouldn't it be cool to be able to create origami on your own without having me here, having to explain it to you?"

"I like origami. I like making butterflies the best. I know how to make a monarch butterfly. I want to make a butterfly. I want to make a monarch butterfly."

"I totally get it, Bethany. I'm going to make it so you can create a monarch butterfly whenever you want, okay?"

I rummage through Bethany's school bag, but I don't find what I'm looking for. I was thinking for sure Bethany had her own cell phone. What teenager *doesn't* have a phone? But I don't see it anywhere.

"Hey, Beth, where's your phone?" I ask her.

"I don't have a phone. *'Bethany, a phone is a bad idea. Someone will probably just steal your phone because you can't keep an eye on it.'* That's what my mom always tells me. But Miss Karen has a phone. I can use Miss Karen's phone if I need one."

"No, no, it's okay, Miss Karen's not even here. Let me see... What else will work for this?" I scan the room to see what I could use for my project. "Wait! I have an iPad that'll work. I'll just have to change my plan a bit. Let me see... Where did I put it?" I mumble to myself.

"The iPad is kept on the top shelf. It only goes on the top shelf, not the bottom shelf. Alyssa can reach the bottom shelf but not the top. We don't want Alyssa getting the iPad on the bottom shelf," Bethany announces, capturing her mother's tone of voice perfectly once more.

"Yes, I know that at your house the iPad is kept on the high shelf. But at my house I don't always put things away in the right place..." I trail off as I start flinging clothes off my desk chair in the hope that my iPad is hiding under there. No luck. I look in my desk drawers and in my closet, but don't find it. Finally, I reach up to the top shelf of my bookcase, and sure enough, feel my fingers graze the metallic edge of the iPad. Sometimes Bethany seems to be telepathic or something.

My initial thought is to just use the sound recording app that comes with the iPad, but then I figure if Bethany's going to be using this, it might be helpful for her mom to see the steps so she can help out, if need be. I decide YouTube is my best bet.

I plop myself back on the floor in front of the bed and get to work. Before long, I've created a random account on YouTube, and I'm setting the iPad up behind me on the bed. I have it perched between two of my stuffies, and the camera is pointing down, over my shoulder and into the space right in front of me. I've placed a pile of white paper there, and my legs straddle the paper on either side, so they're not in view of the camera.

My idea—I'm going to make YouTube videos of me creating a bunch of origami masterpieces so Bethany can log in at any time to learn how to make them, even if I'm not with her. I feel like my idea is brilliant, and I'm super-excited that I can do this for her. I double-check that the camera's view only gets a shot of my hands as they fold and crease. There is no way I want my face or body in any part of this video.

When I'm satisfied things are set up perfectly, I double-check that Bethany is still immersed in her audiobook so she won't interrupt me. Then I hit *record*.

"Hi, there. This is origami tutorial number one, the monarch butterfly. I hope you enjoy."

I go on to explicitly describe each step of the process, my fingers expertly folding and creasing along with each component. Five minutes later I hold the delicate creation up to the camera and announce, "Voilà...a monarch butterfly."

I laugh to myself as I review this first video, because it reminds me of the YouTube videos Amy and Anna are always watching that my mom absolutely *hates*. There's this lady who has an entire YouTube empire based on little kids all over the world watching her open Kinder Surprise eggs. Yeah, crazy, right? You can't see her face in the videos, and they are literally just videos of her opening those crappy little eggs you get at Easter. I have *no* idea why a five-year-old would be into that, but sure enough, Amy and Anna turn into zombies when they start watching those videos. It's like crack for little kids. *So weird...* My mom even offered to buy them a Costco-sized pack of Kinder Surprises they could open themselves if they promise never to watch the videos again. Which, in my mind, is even crazier. *Come on, Mom! Who's the parent, after all?*

I'm having so much fun creating the tutorials that time passes much more quickly than I realize. As I'm about to start my seventh installment—a crocodile—I hear Mom calling up to tell me that Bethany's mom is here to pick her up. I grab her hand—which is pretty normal for us now—to lead her down the stairs and to the front door. My mom chats with Mrs. Robertson for a few minutes and I take the opportunity to run upstairs to grab the origami creations I've just made. I figure I may as well give them to Bethany right now, and maybe it'll make it easier for her when she's making her own.

When I get back downstairs, I'm eager to start telling Mom and Mrs. Robertson about my idea for the YouTube tutorial for Bethany.

"Well, doesn't that sound like an incredible idea? How thoughtful of you!" remarks Bethany's mom. "It'll be great to have that on while I'm cooking dinner. Bethany, you can sit at the dining table and listen to Jodie teach you how to make new creations while I'm in the kitchen. Or on rainy days when Karen and you can't go outside for a walk, it'll give you something to do!"

"I make origami butterflies. And today Jodie taught me how to make a crocodile and a frog and an elephant. 'This frickin' ear won't fold properly,'" Bethany repeats under her breath, just the way I had accidentally blurted it out upstairs when we were in my room. We had to delete that video.

"Sorry, Mrs. Robertson. Sometimes I forget that Bethany is so...impressionable," I apologize, embarrassed that Bethany has repeated this in front of our parents. It makes me wonder what other phrases she's repeated. I make a mental note not to talk out loud to her anymore if I'm saying anything I'd rather keep private.

"Oh, don't even worry about it. I'm sure you've heard Bethany repeat way worse from her father and me. I have to admit that it keeps a person in check, though, to hear all of the nasty words we say repeated right back to us!"

I'm tempted to jump into a retelling of the Sean Fedun incident right here, but I hold back. I've been much more open lately, and I've felt a lot more comfortable talking to Mom about stuff. But, I'm not sure she's ready to hear that I've basically shut down any opportunity to join the Kayla–Sean friendship group. I think she's still holding out hope that I will break into becoming a sprite one day.

After Bethany and her mom leave, I grab one of the new books I've taken out of the library and snuggle in on the living room couch. Normally, I'd head back to my room, but Mom is in the middle of making cinnamon buns and the warm scent floating in from the kitchen has wrapped the entire main floor of the house in a comforting, spice-scented blanket. As I relax into the cushions, I'm surprised when Amy plops down beside me. She has grabbed one of her princess picture books and, as she starts flipping the pages, I feel her weight gently press into my legs, which are curled up beneath me. Soon, Anna wanders in too. She's holding one of her Barbies and sits cross-legged on the floor in front of me. She begins to methodically brush out Barbie's long blonde hair. Without thinking about what I'm doing, I half sit up and reach toward her.

"Here... Let me show you how to braid," I say gently over her shoulder. I separate Barbie's hair into three sections then guide Anna's hands, one over the other, until a long, thick braid snakes from Barbie's head. Together, we secure the braid with an elastic and Anna jumps up to go and show Mom what she's learned to do. I finger the braids on my own head and can't help but notice that my heart feels a little fuller today.

Chapter Eighteen

Today is Tuesday — the first Tuesday of the month, in fact. But I don't dread it quite as much as I used to.

My mom settles down in the oversized nylon chair across from Mr. Rutter, impatient to hear about how my life in high school is turning right around. He starts in with his accolades about my academic achievements, if one can even call them that.

"So, Sandra, I've spoken to Ms. Kelly, and apparently Jodie has been doing very well in language arts class lately. Very well indeed. I hear that they've been working on a poetry unit and Jodie has turned out to be a bit of a star student." He smiles at me and his eyes twinkle, and I feel, I don't know, *proud* that he's bragging about me. Because I guess I know what he's saying is the truth. I am really good at this poetry stuff.

I like that the rules can be stretched and twisted, like a ball of silly putty. I have the freedom to say what I think and feel without having to worry about things completely making sense — well, at least to anyone other than me. But Ms. Kelly dropped a bit of a bomb on us yesterday. She's been teaching us the different figures of speech and we've had to create poems that focus on personification, alliteration and all of the other 'ation' words I can't keep track of. And this has all been fine and kind of fun even, because no one has ever had to *read* any of my poems.

But yesterday, she announced to the class that on Friday we're going to have to choose our very favorite figures of speech poem and read it to the class. I was sitting there doodling on my paper, lost in a world that included Jared, me and a whole lot of double fudge ice cream, when I just froze.

I don't do public presentations of *any* kind. My mind raced back to 'the incident' then to the outing of me in the *Annie* choir rehearsal — all of the things that put me at the center of attention. I had the sudden urge to bolt from the classroom. I kept thinking, *if there is any way I can get out of this, any way at all, I will do it.* I tried to make up excuses in my head that would sound legit and I even counted back the days to my last period in case that was the excuse I would have to use.

Then I thought, *Mom got me out of auditions for the play. Why can't she get me out of this?*

"Mom, I can't read my poem in front of the class. I think I will literally throw up all over the entire ninth grade if I stand up there. Do you really want me in that situation again? Are you wanting to torture me?"

"Oh, Jodie, don't be so dramatic. This is not a big deal and you will be just fine. This poem presentation will give the other kids a chance to see just how bright and creative you are. We've been talking about improving your confidence level and this sounds like the perfect opportunity. Eugene...your thoughts?"

It is not lost on me that she uses Mr. Rutter's first name. I don't know… Does she think that'll give her an edge with him? Like they are best buddies on the same team? Or it could be flirting. Oh God, is she flirting with my counselor?

Whatever she thinks she's doing, it's working, because Mr. Rutter lets out a deep sigh, leans back in his chair and turns his attention to me with a soft look on his face.

"Jodie, I'm afraid I have to agree with your mom on this one. I think you've made huge gains with your confidence and social acceptance, and I think this is a great opportunity for you to test yourself even further. If you can do this, Jodie, I think you're ready for almost anything. In fact, I'm not sure we'd need to have any more of these little check-ins…at all."

No more constant scrutinizing by my mother and the guidance counselor? No more meetings where my every action is put under a microscope? Nothing sounds better than that, even though I am sick at the prospect of what I need to do in order to earn that privilege.

I think about what it'll take for me to be up there in front of everyone — my heart racing, face blushing, sweat pouring in between my breasts. Thirty pairs of eyes will be staring right at me, and everyone will have judgy looks on their faces. Just the thought of reading my own personal feelings to a group of students I don't necessarily know, never mind *like*, makes my heart race and my lungs collapse.

"Okay, fine. I guess. But if I get up there and do this, both of you promise that you'll just let me be from now on? No more weekly check-ins and constant meddling?" I glance from my mom to Mr. Rutter and back again, so they know that I mean it, and that I mean both of them.

"Yep, we agree," Mom and Mr. Rutter — aka 'Eugene' — answer in tandem.

Okay. Fine. I guess I'm doing this. Then I'm free — free of all this shit and I can just go back to being me.

But in the back of my mind I know that it's not just the standing up in front of the class that I'm stressed about.

No, the real problem — the part that makes my stomach turn and my head swim — is what I'm supposed to read when I'm up there. Ms. Kelly inspired us to write poetry that is *raw and honest and heartfelt*, so that's what I did, because I didn't think it would ever leave my notebook. But the thought of saying those words aloud? Well, it's unimaginable.

I decide now might be the only time I have a chance to bring this up with both Mr. Rutter and my mom. And now might be my best chance at any empathy.

"Mr. Rutter, I know you want me to be all confident and everything. But what happens if the thing you present to the class isn't super-cool for the other kids to hear? What if it just makes me get judged even more harshly? Bullied even more cruelly?"

"What are you talking about, Jodie?" my mom chimes in.

"It's just that... Well...the stuff I have to say might be a little awkward for some people to hear." I realize that I am being vague and that their minds are probably scanning through a list of the worst popular topics a poem could be about. Sex? Suicide? Teen pregnancy?

I don't want them to flip out or ask to see the poem, so I try to backpedal a little.

"It's nothing super-bad. I'm not in trouble or going to harm myself or anything. My poem just might be a little difficult for some kids to hear."

I see Mom and Mr. Rutter both relax visibly as I reassure them that I am not in any type of immediate crisis. They totally must have thought my poem was a suicide note! *So much for trusting me and all my gains this year.*

"I'm just wondering… What do I do if the topic I'm writing about isn't super-cool to some people? Should I scrap that poem and scramble to write another?"

Mr. Rutter jumps in before my mom has a chance to talk. "Well, no, Jodie. That would be censoring, and our country's First Amendment guarantees the freedom of speech for all individuals. You are allowed to express your opinions, your perspectives and your ideations, free from persecution. We have just told you that we believe your values and opinions are important and we want you to have enough self-confidence that you can always be free to be who you want to be, whether it's easily accepted by others or not."

Mr. Rutter shoots a steely look at my mom, silently urging her to offer some sort of motherly advice.

"Um, well, yes. I would agree with Mr. Rutter. We will support you in whatever you do, Jodie, even if you create a few waves while you're doing it." She glances at Mr. Rutter, probably attempting to get a sense of approval from him.

I guess I'm not the only one in the family who constantly doubts her social interactions.

As if to reiterate her point, Mom reaches over and squeezes my hand, like she's placing a final cherry on top. Then she takes a deep breath and goes on.

"Jodie, we just want you to know how very proud of you we are. Three months ago, you never would have felt comfortable sharing things with us, making new friends, standing in front of the class to recite anything, never mind something that you wrote yourself! This change in confidence has been so refreshing. It's been great to see you…well…*happy*." She says it tentatively, as if the word is a delicate egg and she's gently placing it on the counter, anxious that it might wobble, roll off and smash to the ground.

"I totally agree with your mom, Jodie. You seem to be putting more effort into your studies, you're taking more care in your appearance and I don't worry about you spending so much time alone. I feel like maybe Bethany and Miss Karen may have something to do with it?" Mr. Rutter's eyes find mine dead-on, and they feel like laser beams shooting X-rays right through to my bones.

"Yeah, I guess I'm feeling better lately. Good, even. And school isn't so terrible anymore. Hanging out with Bethany has been cool. And my new friend Jared has been pretty cool too." I shift my eyes to Mom to measure her reaction when I mention a boy's name. I'm pleasantly surprised that she remains cool and unfazed.

"And, I don't know, I guess I just feel like I don't really care so much about everyone else."

This time I turn to look squarely at my mom.

"I don't care about Kayla, or Sean, or any of those people who make my life miserable, Mom. And I wish you didn't care so much either. I know you want me to fit in and be popular, and date, and cheer and all of that stuff. But that's not me. I don't want that. I don't want any of that." And I can't believe that as soon as the words come out of my mouth, about a twenty-pound weight is lifted off my body. I'm suddenly feeling so much lighter and freer that I'm dying to check whether my clothes have suddenly gotten a bit loose on me too.

"You know what, Jodie? I'm starting to get that too. And I want you to know that I like who you are. No, let me try that again. I *love* who you are, no matter where you belong. I don't care about who you fit in with or what you do. I just want to see you happy, Jodie. I've really enjoyed seeing you happy this last while." And this time when she says the word *happy*, it is loud and free and full of hope. And through her eyes, I can tell my mom actually *sees* me for the first time.

We say our goodbyes to Mr. Rutter, and, true to his word, he says he'll probably only want to see me once more before the end of the year. He wishes me luck on my poetry reading and lets me know that he's got my back, no matter what. I'm elated with this newfound freedom and independence, but I must admit that I'm a little terrified too. Mr. Rutter has always been my number-one supporter, the person who seemed to get me, even when no one else did. Tackling the rest of the year's challenges without his constant support and guidance might be more than I can handle. And what about next year? I've finally figured out how to survive ninth grade, but I've got three more years of high school left and the rules seem to be constantly changing. What if I can't adapt like I'm supposed to? Am I going to have to start things all over again every September?

My brain is still filled with all my pressing anxieties as I walk down the hallway to math class. I turn to cut through the atrium when I see a group of seventh-grade students from the adjoining middle school huddled around a table. At first, I think maybe there's a fight, then I wonder if they're doing drugs or something. They're standing so close together that I can't really see what's happening in the middle. I'm surprised that one of the teachers hasn't come by and split them up yet. As I approach, I notice that they're watching something on one of the girl's iPads, and it seems like there's a giant heap of crumpled paper in the middle of the table. I try to inch my way closer without drawing too much attention to myself. I peel my backpack off, place it down in front of me and pretend to be searching for something inside. When I glance up, I'm able to look through a space where the shoulders of two of the girls aren't quite touching. It takes me by surprise to find that they aren't doing anything inappropriate at all. The pile of so-called trash is actually a collection of origami creations, like the ones I do—the ones I've kept hidden in my room for years so that I'm not made fun of.

As long as I've been going to this school, I've never seen anyone doing origami for fun. I've always been pretty confident that I'm the only one who geeks out that badly. And my body all of a sudden feels like it's going to explode in panic.

There's one girl in the center of the group, unmistakable with her golden hair and tanned skin. It's Sean Fedun's younger sister Jess, who is definitely a sprite in the making, if only in seventh grade. Unlike other students who make their way through middle school feeling like Bambi on an ice rink, I remember Jess Fedun walking in like she owned the place—like she already belonged, even before she started. I guess that's what happens when you have a jerk of an older brother who has brainwashed you into thinking he's king and you're the next big thing.

As I peek through the space in the huddle, I see Jess ping-ponging her eyes between the iPad and a sheet of paper she has in front of her on the table. I freeze with my breath held, because I know those folds so well. *Inside reverse fold one side, inside reverse fold the other, then carefully fold down the wings.*

Then I hear it. Without a doubt, my own voice coming from the iPad. *"And this is how you make a paper swan."*

I'm momentarily perplexed, like I can't quite grasp how *my voice* can be on *her iPad.* It feels like some sort of hoax someone is playing on me. But I look around, and no one is paying any attention to me. They are all so focused on the origami tutorial that they have no idea I've even stopped to stare.

My mind flashes back to the last week, when Bethany and I sat in my room and I put together the videos for her. Then I think about how I spent each day since adding more videos to the YouTube channel. It seemed like such a good idea, a great way for Bethany to be able to join me in my world, for us to connect. I didn't for one second think anyone else in the world would take notice. I think back to the privacy controls I failed to implement, about how I never thought they'd be needed and about how my mom questioned me about whether I'd really thought this through. I've spent my entire first year of high school without more than a handful of people even knowing I've *existed,* never mind being interested in what I've been doing. And now they're watching me on YouTube?

Before I get too panicked, I remember that my face isn't visible anywhere on the screen. *I made sure of that, didn't I?* And considering no one even talks to me, I can't imagine they would recognize my voice.

I decide to ditch the remainder of math class and instead run to the nearest bathroom. I lock myself in a stall and pull out my phone. I find it ironic that I happen to have chosen the same stall I discovered Kayla and Sean in that one day. Funny that I was a fly on the wall in their world, never thinking that there would ever be flies peering into my own world.

Then I look up at the door of the stall and see that has been scratched over with Sharpie a thousand times by someone full of rage and hurt.

Mrs. Kelly is a cow.
Go Sabers Go!
Roses are red, violets are blue, you are so nasty, I see you taking a poo.
Love the life you live. Live the life you love. — *Bob Marley*

And that Bob Marley quote seems to speak a different language to me suddenly. *Live the life I love.* I can do that. I *am* doing that. Now. Finally.

I pull up my YouTube channel, hold my breath, count to three then snap my eyes open to see what I fear most.

Twenty-four hundred and seventy-one views.

Nine hundred and eighty-two likes.

That's more people than I think I've ever met in my life. The video goes on to play after I pull it up and I cringe when I hear my voice. *Why did I think this was such a good idea?* I contemplate taking it down straight away, but then I hesitate.

Really, in terms of an online presence, that number of views is basically nothing — a number smaller than the followers Kayla probably has on her Instagram account. Not even a blip on the Internet radar. I feel like maybe it's just a fluke that a few people have stumbled across the videos, and no one will even remember them by tomorrow. Yeah, that's it. I'll just stay quiet and it'll all disappear. After all, it's not like anyone can tell it's me, right?

I take a couple more deep breaths then let myself out of the bathroom stall. I'm good at putting on a stone face and today is no exception.

For the rest of the day, I refuse to even think about the origami situation. I've got too much already on my mind with the poem I'm working on for Friday. Ms. Kelly gives us the entire class to work on it this afternoon, and we're able to buddy up so that someone else can help us revise and edit.

Bethany is away today at a doctor's appointment, but Miss Karen is still in class to help the teacher. I know I can trust her opinion of my poem, but I sit with a bubbling storm in my stomach as I watch her read it in front of me.

"Wow, Jodie. This is really good. And I love that it's honest and straight from the heart. But are you sure you want to do this? It's pretty gutsy."

"I know. I'm sorta surprised myself. But I feel like I can do this. I mean, how much worse can it get for me? Maybe this will put him in his place?"

"As long as you're good with the possible repercussions, I think it's brilliant. And I must admit that it'll be pretty funny when Bethany ends up putting these words on repeat for the next couple of weeks." We laugh, thinking about how Bethany will mimic my poem and how she'll say the words with such vigor over and over. The meaning will reverberate through the hallways.

The bell finally rings, and we file out of class. My mind has been so wrapped around my poem for the last hour that I haven't thought about the YouTube channel at all. That is, until I stride through the hallway and see Zoe and Kayla attempting to glide folded paper swans to each other, like airplanes zooming through the hallway. They giggle and joke, each time picking one off the floor, re-bending the wings and trying again.

Sean saunters down the hallway, and, without even looking at her, calls out to Kayla.

"Are you coming, babe?"

"Huh?" she replies. "No, remember? Zoe and I are hanging out today. We can hang out tomorrow, though."

"You and Zoe can hang out another day. My parents are working late, which means we get the house to ourselves. I want you to come over. Let's go," he insists.

"No, Sean. I made plans with Zoe. I can come over to your house tomorrow, okay?" She tries to stand her ground, but you can see by the pleading look in her eyes that her response is more of a request than a statement.

"I said we're going over to my place today. Come on." He gives her a steely look and grabs her arm to lead her through the hall. Kayla pulls back for just a moment then looks back at Zoe and shrugs her shoulders.

"Sorry, Zoe. I forgot I promised Sean I'd hang out today. We'll do it again another day, okay?"

"Yeah, whatever. Go hang out with Sean." Zoe turns around sharply and focuses her attention on Rebecca, who has stood there silently throughout the entire conversation. I hear Zoe mumble the word 'asshole' under her breath and see her roll her eyes.

When I turn to see if Kayla and Sean have heard, I see his arm snake around her waist and pull her close to him, so they are walking side by side. I see her scooch over a bit and try to walk on her own, but his grip is firm and it's leaving faint imprints on the sliver of skin visible between the waist of her jeans and her cropped shirt. He tries to nuzzle in and kiss her neck, but even from this angle I see the look of absolute resignation on her face. As they continue to walk in time with each other, Kayla's foot strikes one of the paper swans that have been left lying on the laminate flooring. I see its wing crumple and tear, the bird unable to take flight again. At this moment, I wonder — *How glorious is it really to be Kayla Sutton after all?*

Chapter Nineteen

As has been the routine for the last couple of days, I roll over in bed and the first thing I do when I wake up is pick up my phone. I don't scroll through Twitter or Instagram or Facebook like most other fifteen-year-olds. No, I don't even have social media accounts, to tell the truth. I head straight to my YouTube channel to check the damage. My *fan base*, if I can call it that, has grown steadily through the week and it's got me feeling totally anxious all the time. I mean, it doesn't seem like anyone has clued in that it's actually *me*, but it feels like the secret is a giant balloon getting more and more air blown into it with every passing day, although I'm never quite sure when it's going to explode. I worry constantly that I'm going to jump with the deafening sound of this massive balloon popping in my face.

Yesterday's total was nearly fourteen thousand views, and just over eight thousand likes. I cringe when I look into my phone this morning and gasp at the number. *How could things have snowballed so out of control? Almost one hundred thousand views?* I don't even know how that's possible!

I head downstairs in a trance, wondering what I should do. I suppose I could take down the videos altogether, but I almost feel like that might bring on more attention at this point. I thought for sure the trend would just fizzle out, but that doesn't seem to be happening. Yesterday at lunch, I noticed another couple of seventh-graders sitting in the hallway attempting a bouquet of origami roses. They were making a mess of it, honestly, and part of me wanted to jump in and show them what they were doing wrong. But obviously that would have been disastrous, so I've been keeping to myself and trying to just go about the week as usual.

I'm sitting in our breakfast nook eating a piece of toast with peanut butter when my mom suddenly turns up the news program she has on.

"Hey, Jodie, have you seen this? It made me think about you. It looks like you've been ahead of the times with all of your origami projects over the past few years."

I look up to the TV to see what she's referring to, and I see my hands on the screen and hear my unmistakable, pathetically horrible voice blaring from the TV screen. Luckily Mom has stepped out of the room to pack the girls' backpacks, otherwise I'm positive she would make out that it's me.

The news anchors are doing one of those human-interest pieces that they save for the end of the broadcast. *Trends of the Day* is what they call it. And today the trend is apparently me.

"Trending today we have these online origami videos that have recently gone viral. This anonymous trendsetter has

made quite the splash online, with people all over the world following her origami tutorials. I think you'll agree with me that it's quite astonishing to watch these origami creations come to life right before our eyes. This girl is incredibly talented at what she is able to do." The video feed shifts again from the news anchors to a video of a pair of hands, *my* hands, intricately folding and pressing the edges of paper together to create a beautiful lily. There is no sound to the video clip this time, but you can hear the anchor woman's voiceover, speaking to her male counterpart.

"Kurt, have you seen anything quite like this? I find I can't stop watching. It's like watching endless clips of those cats playing piano on YouTube." They both do that fake chuckle thing that news people always do, then continue. *"You just can't turn away. My thirteen-year-old daughter got me hooked last night and we've been working on making the elephant piece ever since. Although I have to admit, mine doesn't look quite as perfect as the ones in the video."*

They both chuckle one more time, then the news program switches to a sports story about the latest golf tournament. My mom walks back into the kitchen, turns off the TV and goes back to making our lunches, completely oblivious to the fact that my world has just tilted completely upside down.

For a moment all time stops. It's like my mind and body numb and I'm unable to gather my thoughts. My mom goes about her business in the kitchen, apparently unaware that the person on the screen was me. She calls over her shoulder.

"Have you seen those videos, Jodie? I guess they're super-popular right now. And here you've been doing it all along! Forget that girl! You could create your own videos and be a superstar!" She laughs like it's the funniest thing in the world and I pretend that the peanut butter in my mouth prevents me from responding.

I'm on the frickin' news now? What is happening with my life? Just a few weeks ago I was a quiet wallflower who floated through life like a tiny speck of dust — unnoticed and unattached. Now I feel like my cloak of invisibility has been ripped from me and I'm standing naked on the world's stage.

Of course, there's still the possibility that no one knows it's me. But I have to at least come to terms with the fact that at some point they will find out. Then what? Will I be the target of even more harassment? Will there be cruel memes and online jokes circling around me that I'll have to dodge, like icy snowballs coming at my face?

I need to talk to somebody about this. I need to vent and let it all out. But who can I trust? Who will protect my secret?

My first thought is, of course, Mr. Rutter. But I made it clear last Tuesday that I was no longer interested in his constant meddling or advice. I can't exactly come in two days later, begging for his help in solving a problem. No, he would probably just report it all to Mom anyway, and I know she wouldn't understand.

My next thought is Bethany, but it's no surprise that keeping secrets is just not her jam. It's true that she won't go crazy and judgy on me, and she probably wouldn't even understand what it means to *go viral*. In fact, I don't think she would think it's a big deal at all. But with her lack of filter, there's too great a chance that she'll just blurt something out in the middle of class, and all eyes will be on me.

My mind then shifts to Jared — to his gentle nature, his indifference to social norms or to any high-school drama whatsoever. Yeah, I can trust Jared. He'll know what to do.

I look at the clock. I can't exactly text him first thing in the morning. I mean, he'll be rushing out the door to school.

But wait. No, I guess he won't be heading to school since his house *is* his school. And it's Thursday morning. I know he's mentioned that he loves Thursday mornings because his mom takes his brother to an early morning physical therapy appointment and he doesn't have to work, so he gets to sleep in a bit. I think about the classes I have this morning — science and art. Really, not a big deal to miss, especially seeing as Mr. Hutchins is giving us another study period to prepare for our test on chemical reactions next week. Yeah, this situation is way more important than a study period and an art class.

I hastily grab my bag and fly through the front door, so my mom thinks I'm in a rush to get to school. I think I remember how to get to Jared's house, as we stopped by there one day before we went to the library. He lives in a cozy duplex about halfway between the school and my place. It would be way faster to take the bus, but I'm so full of adrenaline that I figure walking will allow me to clear my head. I text him on the way to let him know I'm popping by and hope that I'm putting my trust in the right person.

A half an hour later I walk up his cracked front steps, a little sweaty and disheveled from my urgent race here. Strands of my hair have snuck their way out of my ponytail and plastered themselves with sweat on either side of my face. At least I had the sense to wear leggings and a T-shirt today, so my legs aren't as clammy and chaffed as they would be if I was in a skirt or shorts. But I am keenly aware that my back probably has a sweat mark the size of a dinner plate underneath where my backpack has been sitting, and never mind my breasts. I can almost imagine the pool of sweat that has built up in my cleavage, threatening to drip all the way down my belly. I give my armpits a quick sniff, just to make sure I am not entirely revolting. But I am a mess…in every possible way.

Despite all of this, I ring Jared's doorbell. Because, to be honest, I am desperate and I need someone to help me get out of this disaster. And to think that I once thought 'the incident' was the worst possible thing to happen to me. That seems like nothing compared to the entire world finding out how much of a geeky loser I am. I need someone to tell me it's not bad, because all my brain is telling me these days is, *It really is that bad…*

The lights are all off in the house, but I figure it just means he's been hanging in his room. I wait a few minutes for him to answer the door before I ring again. He hasn't responded to my texts that I was coming, so I'm suddenly worried he's out and this has been a massive waste of time.

I'm about to try to text him one more time when the door swings open and he's standing in front of me in a pair of pajama pants hanging dangerously low on his hips and with no shirt on.

I'm caught off guard and a little breathless, as I assumed he'd be dressed. I mean, who answers the front door without clothes on? I don't even leave my bathroom without being fully clothed.

I try not to stare, but the expanse of bare skin in front of me makes it impossible for me to look anywhere else.

I've never really thought much before about seeing Jared naked. I haven't really thought much about seeing anyone naked before. I mean, there was that one time when I imagined kissing him in the mirror — okay, maybe the kissing fantasy happened more than once — but in my daydreams, he always had clothes on. I just assumed his body was a bit pale and scrawny, not something you would drool over at eight a.m.!

But the body in front of me now? Well, it's a whole lot better than I expected. He's skinny, sure, but his muscles are sinewy and lean, giving him the look of a professional climber or a yoga instructor or something. I glance up at his face as he runs his hand through his wild and matted hair. It's obvious I've woken him up as there's a crusty bit of dried drool on the corner of his mouth. But even this doesn't do much to dampen my interest. For a split second, all my anxieties melt away and I forget why I'm even standing here.

"Oh, hey, Jodie. What's up? Sorry... I was just sleeping. Isn't it a Thursday? What are you doing here?" As he speaks, he holds open the door and steps back to let me come in. I love that he automatically lets me in, even though he has no clue why I'm at his door at eight a.m.

"I need your help, Jared. I-I'm not sure what to do." My eyes well up with tears and I can see the concern on his face.

"What's going on? Are you okay? Are the twins okay?"

"Yeah, yeah, everybody is fine." Now I'm feeling a bit like maybe I'm overreacting. I mean, no one is hurt or sick or out of a job. This problem is manageable, right?

"I don't know how to explain things. It'll be better if I just show you." He leads me down the hall to the living room and we sit down on his worn leather couch. I'm grateful for the chance to sit, and I relish the cool leather on my back. I dig out my phone from my backpack, log in to my YouTube channel and pass the phone over to him.

"Look."

He takes a few moments to examine my phone scrolling through the videos and playing them every so often. I try to read the expression on his face to see if he sees this as disastrously as I do. But every time I look up at it, my gaze starts to drift downward to his bare chest again — to the smattering of freckles he has across his collarbone, to the smooth paleness of his stomach as he lies back against the armrest of the couch. *Wait! Are those abs? Does he seriously have abs?*

Eventually he looks up at me with a gigantic grin spread across his face.

"Jodie, is this you? Is this seriously *you*? This is so awesome! This is epic! This is like the coolest thing to ever happen! You seriously have your own YouTube channel?"

"Um, well, yeah. I made it for Bethany. Remember, I told you that I was teaching her to make origami? I wanted her to be able to follow along and figured her mom or Karen wouldn't have a clue unless I videoed it. Honestly, I thought she'd be the only one logging in. I didn't know it would turn into such a disaster! I never wanted anyone else to watch it. It was supposed to be private, not seen by over a hundred thousand viewers!"

"A hundred thousand viewers, Jodie? Try close to half a million!" He turns the phone back over to me and I look at the screen in disbelief.

"How did this happen? When I woke up this morning it was only a hundred thousand views. Jared, I don't know what to do. I feel like I'm rolling down a steep hill and with every breath I pick up momentum. I don't know how to stop, and I feel like I'm soon going to crash." I cradle my head in my hands.

"Slow down, Jodie. Take a breath and let's just talk about it." He reaches over and gently pulls my hands from my face. "Honestly, Jodie, I don't see a problem here. No one knows it's you. You're still making the videos for Bethany. It's just that other people get to enjoy them too. Maybe it's time people see how cool you really are."

He then moves his hand from my arm to tuck one of those stray hairs behind my ear. It sends a bolt of electricity through my body and I feel, if only for a moment, like I am the most powerful girl on the planet.

"Jodie, you can make a killing from this, too. Did you know that?"

"What, you mean make money? From posting my videos?"

"Yeah, of course. Haven't you heard of YouTube stars? You could be the next YouTube sensation! Here, I'll show you how to get started. This could literally change your life forever — and in a good way, I promise. You just have to apply to be a member of the YouTube Partner Program. YPP is what they call it. Once they approve you, you can select the types of ads you're okay with and voilà! The money starts rolling in. And trust me… With half a million views already, you're going to get approved in a second. Those advertisers are going to be lined up to get on your channel."

I look at him skeptically. He knows way too much about this whole YouTube thing.

"Yeah, yeah, I get it. I'm a dork," he goes on to admit. "When I was twelve, I thought I could be the next big YouTube gamer. I was super into Fortnite and assumed the entire world wanted to see me play. Didn't work out so well. The only three views I ever got were from my mom, my brother and my cousin in Wisconsin. But I do know how this stuff works."

I reluctantly allow him to fiddle with my YouTube account for a bit, and I have to admit that I'm feeling a bit better. I mean, why was I so freaked out, anyway? Being semi-famous isn't the worst thing. I can handle Sean Fedun and Kayla Sutton and all of them. I really couldn't care less what they think about me. And maybe Jared is right. Maybe the rest of the world needs to see who I really am.

After we talk on the couch for a few more minutes, Jared walks me back to the front door. He offers for me to stay and hang out for the day, but I feel like I should get to my afternoon classes, at the least. Today is our last class to work on the poems we've written, then presentations are tomorrow. I need all the time I can get to polish mine and build my confidence enough to actually read it aloud. Forget about the world seeing who I am… Tomorrow, the entire ninth grade is either going to love me or hate me. I'm not sure which way it's going to go.

After I get my shoes on, I sort of stand there awkwardly in the doorway for a moment, not sure how to say goodbye. Most of the time when Jared and I leave each other, we're at a public place like the yogurt shop or the library. So, we typically just give a dorky high-five and go our separate ways. But I am acutely aware that we are completely alone for the first time right now.

"Well, thanks for making me feel better. I really do — feel better, I mean."

"Honestly, things are going to work out, Jodie. I promise. For most kids, what you've done is a dream come true. I think it's totally cool. I mean, I think you're totally cool."

As he says this, he leans in just a bit and touches me lightly on the shoulder. My heart is racing a mile a minute and I know I must make a split-second decision. I let my body lead my brain for once and I take a step forward as well. I reach my arms up and around to give him a hug goodbye. I can feel his hands wrap around my waist, and for the first time I'm not thinking about the extra rolls I have there or how much of a mess I must look right now.

No. I am too busy feeling the smooth muscles of his back.

Smelling his slightly sweet, slightly musty, just-woken-up scent.

Acknowledging the fact that my boobs are pressed tightly against his bare chest.

His soft breath on the side of my cheek as he turns his face toward me and ever-so-softly kisses me on the mouth.

What the hell is happening? He is kissing me on the mouth. I am being kissed on the mouth right now. By a boy. In real life.

I think back to the hundreds of times I watched Kayla or any of the other sprites flirting with the boys. Touching the boys. Being tickled by one of the boys.

I think back to the episodes of me kissing myself in the mirror, of how I imagined it feeling the day I got to kiss a boy, the day a boy would run his hands through my hair and down my back.

I never imagined it feeling like this.

No, this feels *way* better than I could have imagined. This moment feels amazing, kind of like the feeling I get when I finish the last fold of a swan's wing.

Perfect.

Chapter Twenty

Today is the day—the day that could, and might, ruin me for the rest of my teenage years. But somehow, instead of stressing about the poem I'm going to read or about the nearly *one million* hits on my YouTube channel I awoke to this morning, all I can think about is how Jared's mouth tasted yesterday, the scratchy, stubbly hairs on the back of his neck and the lightning bolts that were firing up deep inside my belly.

It's almost like that kiss with Jared yesterday has given me a superpower, a protective shell that is almost impenetrable. My anxieties have subsided. The gray clouds that permanently hover over my head have temporarily parted enough to let some sunshine through. And hell, I even put a little lip gloss on this morning. I am feeling good...*ish*.

Well, that is until I walk up the front steps of the school and feel like suddenly yesterday's kiss was a distant memory and the threats of today lurk imminently close. *Why did I think this was going to be a good idea?*

As I walk through the crowded halls, I try to talk myself through the negative thoughts that continually threaten to drown me.

I can do this. I can read this poem. Don't worry so much about Sean Fedun. He's just a boy — an arrogant, self-entitled, stupid jerk of a boy. He means nothing to me, and I do not care what he thinks.

I mean, it's not like he even cares what I say or think about him. To him I am nothing. I am invisible. So, this is going to be no big deal. It's not like today will be any different from any other crap day in ninth grade.

Except that it is. Because today is the day when everything has the possibility of changing.

From the moment I step into the school today, everything feels different. Everywhere I look, kids are gathered in small groups throughout the hallways folding and refolding pieces of paper, battling each other to see who can make the master creation. When I glanced at my YouTube account after I woke up this morning, I gawked at the close to a million followers that showed up on my screen. You would think that this would give me a surge of confidence, an air of authority and mystery that I could hold over everyone's head.

But it doesn't.

It just adds to the heavy burden of self-consciousness that weighs down every one of my steps.

Funny enough, no one pays me any notice or gives me any more attention than they ever do. I am simply *Jodie what's-her-name-again? The tall, fat one. You know, the black girl, the ninth-grade dorky wallflower.* Everyone is too busy in their own worlds to notice that mine has turned upside-down.

But I just keep imagining that at any second, one of the other students will look up with recognition in their eyes, shouting and pointing, "It's *her*! Look! It's *her*!" And I will be so unnerved by the discovery that my plan to take down Sean Fedun won't get put into action.

My biggest fear is that my cozy world of anonymity will vanish, and I'm just not ready for that. Not yet.

I'm caught off-guard for a moment with a sudden urge to talk to Bethany. It's like I crave her presence. It would be ideal to have Jared here beside me as a solid support to help me get through the day. But he doesn't go to the school, so that's never going to happen.

Bethany is a pretty good second place. With Bethany, I feel so in control, like I'm the one leading the way. I don't have to worry about what she thinks, because she forms no judgments. I imagine sitting in her room, lost in a world of Stephen King novels and Dave Brubeck piano riffs, with Bethany's hands expertly tackling my frizzy mane. It sends a rush of calm down my spine, and after taking a deep breath, I'm feeling like I can do this.

I wander through the day in a fuzzy haze with only one thought repetitively going through my mind — language arts class. The last block of the day inches closer and closer until it is impossible to avoid. I'm relieved to find that I'm the first one in class, so I sit in my usual chair at the table near the back and pull out a book to read. The farther I can remove myself from existing in this world, the better. I mean, this is my jam. This is what I do. I excuse myself from existence and hide out in my shell until it's safe to return.

Eventually the class starts to fill and every few moments I glance up from my book to see whether *his* seat is filled. Part of me is praying for Sean to be cutting class today, maybe having another little make-out session with Kayla in the bathroom. Then I won't have to feel his icy glare as I stand up there reading my poem.

But another part of me, this tiny, brave part that's just starting to blossom, is actually hoping Sean will saunter in and take his seat, front and center. I want to confront him. I feel ready for it. His tyranny over me has gone on long enough and it is going to stop today.

Right before the bell rings, a flood of students come in and shuffle to their seats before Ms. Kelly shuts the door. Among them are Kayla and Sean, who sit side by side at the table near the front. Even as they sit, he keeps his arm resting on her shoulder, like he wants everyone to know that she belongs to him. She doesn't seem to give him much affection back — or maybe she's just more attuned to the fact that they are now in class and public displays of affection are a little over the top. Regardless, she sits there and lets his hand linger on her shoulder, and it almost looks as though that hand is slowly draining the energy from her, the spark that has always made her Kayla. She just sort of slouches there, not the confident sprite she's known to be.

Rebecca files in after them, and surprisingly doesn't sit at their table like she usually does. Instead, she comes to the back of the room and slides into one of the chairs at my table. Yes, I said that right. She's sitting at *my* table. And it's not like that's the only seat available in class or anything. Granted, she chooses the farthest chair possible from me, but still, it's *my* table. I pretend I'm so engrossed in my book that I don't notice her, when in fact, I am keenly aware of every aspect of her — the fact that she's not wearing a crop-top today like most of the sprites wear. Instead, she wears jeans and a casual hoodie. Her hair has been pulled back into an easy ponytail rather than curled and styled into glossy locks around her shoulders and her face looks fresh and clean, the only hint of makeup being a bit of mascara and some lip gloss.

There's definitely been some sort of transformation going on with Rebecca, and for some reason, the change has me feeling hopeful.

After Rebecca, Bethany and Karen walk through the class. You would think that Bethany would come and sit with me, seeing as we've been hanging out so much, but Karen needs a place for Bethany's brailler, so they automatically go to a special table set up for them at the back of the room. But as they pass, I make sure to call out to Beth, so she knows I'm in class.

"Hey, Beth! How are you? Want to hang out after school today?" I reach out to grab her hand as they walk by, Bethany's cane *tap-tap-tapping* its way through the tables and chairs so she can navigate to the back table.

"That's Jodie McGavin. Hi, Jodie McGavin. I would like you to come over after school today. I have a new playlist I would like to listen to with you. And I would like to swing on the swings in the park. And I would like to braid your hair. Can I feel your hair?" She releases her hand from my grasp and reaches it out, searching for my braids. I gently take hold of her hand with both of mine, guiding it away from my head and giving it a squeeze.

"Not now, but later okay? I promise you can braid my hair after school. But right now, it's LA class, so we need to sit down and be quiet." Karen guides her to her seat and gets her set up on the machine.

I notice that the other students flick us with interested glances and raised eyebrows as if to say, "*Seriously? You guys, like…hang out?*" At one point it would have bothered me, and I would have felt super-self-conscious that I was known as *the girl who hangs with the special-needs kid.* But honestly, it just doesn't bother me anymore. Bethany is way cooler than most of those kids will ever be.

As I turn away from Bethany and am about to open my notebook, Rebecca leans across the table and whispers to me.

"I think it's really cool that you spend time with Bethany. I know it must be difficult, and I think it's a really nice thing to do."

Now I know she probably means this as some type of compliment, but I am totally insulted. It's like she thinks that I'm hanging out with Bethany as some sort of charity case, which isn't true at all. I *like* Bethany. She makes me feel good. And she's kind and funny and talented and smart. *Why the hell is it so difficult for people to see that?*

At first, I'm not sure why Rebecca's comment is creating such a hot fire inside me, I mean, I know she doesn't mean it in a condescending way. But then it hits me.

It's because that's how I imagine other people feel when they hang with *me.*

Like I'm a charity case and they're doing me a good deed. My mind goes to Katie Kepperman's birthday party in sixth grade, and the same feelings of humiliation and isolation rise up in me as I had that day.

I had received an invite to Katie's birthday party — my first invitation to any birthday party ever — and I panicked about it. I remember holding that envelope, pale pink with tiny rainbows in the corner, and not knowing what to do. I desperately wanted to go, was dying to be included as part of the pretty, bubbly group of girls in my class, but I was also terrified. So terrified that I would be inadequate, that I would make a fool of myself, that I wouldn't fit in. So, I crumpled that pretty pink invitation up and buried it in the very bottom of my backpack.

What I didn't count on was that my mom chose Saturday morning to go through my backpack, looking for leftover lunch containers. When she pulled out the invitation, she ripped it open, despite the crumpled and juice-stained edges, and she was elated. I don't know if I had ever seen my mom so excited about something going on with *me*. She was, in fact, so overjoyed at the thought that I had been invited to a birthday party that she refused to acknowledge that every girl in our sixth-grade class had been invited to Katie Kepperman's birthday party.

Looking back, I suppose part of the reason for her exuberance could have been the fact that she was scheduled to attend a baby event put on by the Twins and Triplets and More association — yes, that is a thing — and me having my own party meant I was going to be out of her hair for the day.

But we only had an hour until the party, not enough time to run to the store to get a gift and a card. I thought I could use this as another reason not to go, but my mom wasn't to be dissuaded so easily. She recommended that I just whip up a little origami creation to give as a gift.

"Oh, Jodie, everyone loves to receive something homemade," she explained. "You are so talented with that origami. Katie would be thrilled to get a gift made especially for her."

And it's true that people did seem to love receiving my origami presents. I often sent Granny Deans something special for her birthday, and the twins were always delighted when I came up with something new.

So, the dutiful daughter that I was, I disappeared to my room and twenty minutes later I emerged with a breathtaking bouquet of paper lilies and roses, tied together with a pink ribbon. I knew it was doubtful this would pass as a gift, but I didn't have the energy or the gall to argue with my mom, so I didn't have much of a choice.

Mom dropped me off at Katie's house a half-hour after that, with my hair pulled back in a headband, a jean skirt and turquoise T-shirt on, and I stood on her front porch holding my breath, prepared for the worst. But when Katie opened the door, she beamed at my homemade bouquet and ushered me inside. For an entire fifteen minutes, I was like a celebrity with everyone 'oohing' and 'awing' about my creation, asking me how I made them and whether I could teach them. I enjoyed my moment in the sun, but the gaggle of girls soon tired of talking about the exact folds of pieces of paper, and the conversation turned to popstar celebrities and cute boys instead. I slunk back into the corner, my cloak of invisibility spread across me once more, and I counted down the minutes until my mom rang the doorbell and I was able to leave.

It's been a long time since that day in sixth grade, but I've never forgotten that feeling I had sitting there in the corner while all the other girls were playing and chatting so effortlessly. The feeling that I was a forced invitation, a pity one. After that day, I vowed that I would never be the pity invitee again. I would rather spend every day alone than feel like they were doing me a favor by spending time with me.

Like Rebecca Sherman is probably doing right now as she sits at my pity table near the back of the room.

I turn abruptly to her with more venom spewing from me than is probably necessary.

"It is not *nice* of me to spend time with Bethany. And it is not *difficult*, either. Bethany is my friend, and out of every person in this hellhole of a school, she's who I *choose* to hang out with."

I can tell I've surprised her by lashing out, and maybe it is a little much, but with the stress of the YouTube videos and the poetry reading, this comment just knocks me over the top. Rebecca's face turns scarlet and she mumbles an apology then looks down at her notebook. I'm about to apologize myself to try to make things right. After all, this is the girl who I actually want to spend more time with, and I've maybe just ruined my chances.

But before I have an opportunity to say anything, Ms. Kelly claps her hands to get everyone's attention then goes on to give us the details of today's lesson.

"Hello, students, and good afternoon. Looks like everyone is eager for today's class to get started. I'm really excited, myself. I know you're going to blow me away with your creativity. I'm just going to draw popsicle sticks to determine the order in which you'll read. When it's your turn, please come to the front of the class, tell us the name of your poem and a little bit about why you wrote it. Then you can go ahead and share your thoughts with us. We all know that it can be very intimidating to come to the front and read our personal thoughts to the class, so know that this will be a safe and positive environment for you to do so."

She shifts over to her desk where she has a cup full of popsicle sticks with our names written on them.

My stomach feels like an elevator that has plummeted to the basement and I can't quite get my breathing regular. *Oh God, why did I think this was going to be a good idea?*

"And the first to recite their poem today is Mia Perkins."

Mia is a tall, lanky girl who plays on the school's basketball, volleyball and soccer teams. She casually strides to the front of the class like this is no big deal at all and takes her time unfolding a crumpled piece of paper from her back pocket. She goes on to read a pretty lame poem about how a free throw is like a rocket ship, but the comparison is weak at best.

After she's done, Ms. Kelly calls out Nick Papadopoulos, then Aiden Wilke and Jonah Simmons. Each time a new name is called I wince, as if someone is about to poke me with a giant needle. It's getting toward the end of class and I'm half-hoping the bell will save me and I won't have to go after all. But that will just prolong the waiting, my anxiety will flood into next week, and I'll have to do this all over again.

So eventually, third from last, she pulls out a popsicle stick and announces *Jodie McGavin*. I almost hear a cumulative *whoosh* as thirty heads swoop in my direction at the back of the classroom. I'm sure most of the kids don't know who I am and have never really noticed me back there. The others definitely know me, but as the butt of their jokes, the person who helps them feel better about themselves.

I take the piece of paper with the poem written on it out of my notebook and hold it loosely in my hand as I make my way into a standing position. It's like every muscle in my body is fighting me, like my body is telling me not to do this. The loose-leaf makes a flapping sound as it bangs against my leg with every step I take to the front of the room. I've memorized every word of the poem, so it's not like I need to be reading it. But I figure it'll help my nerves to hold something while I'm up there. It's a good thing I've got it all memorized, as the sheet of paper feels almost soggy with the amount of sweat seeping from my palm.

I try to avoid any eye contact as I walk through the tables of students. But as I get near the front, I can't help but look up to Sean Fedun. I know what his expression will be before I even see him. A cocky smirk plasters his face, as if he's set up this whole thing and he's ready to make the entire class laugh at my expense. Kayla is looking at me too, but her face is expressionless — a sort of bored resignation, like she can't wait for this period to be over. She's already recited her poem — one about how dancing is like a rainbow or some cheesy line like that. She obviously doesn't realize that my world is going to forever change in just a few moments.

I look over at Bethany, who is oblivious to the moment of terror I'm experiencing. And for the first time, I'm almost jealous of her. The fact that she never has to see the judging looks on other people's faces, her ability to glide through life not worrying about every single social interaction, like I always do… I envy her ability to appreciate only what she's doing at that exact moment, without second-guessing its impact on the past or the future. She avoids the drama that high school conjures up, and consequently, high school drama eludes her. And typically because of this, Bethany is mostly just left alone. I think about how much better life is when you're left alone, about how hard I've worked at pretending I don't exist.

But then I also think about what Bethany has to deal, with every day, how every little thing she does needs to be done differently because the world is designed for sighted people to navigate. Bethany has a completely different perspective on almost every aspect of life because she perceives life through a different lens. It makes me recognize that, disability or not, we all experience the world from only one vantage point...our own. And I'm starting to think that maybe we need to start craning our necks a little to capture a different point of view. For a moment, I wonder if Bethany ever feels like she's missing out, but then I stop and think, *maybe I'm the one who is missing out? Maybe Bethany's the one with the clearest perspective of all of us?*

My eyes wander past Bethany to Miss Karen, who is looking at me with eager anticipation and urging me on with kind eyes and that warm smile. And I remember what she told me before about not fitting in, but then finding herself and finding her tribe. I take a deep breath and I jump off the cliff. I begin.

"Why Sean Is Like a Butter Knife
By Jodie McGavin

Sean is like a butter knife because he'll stab you in the back until you bleed dry.

Sean is like a butter knife because he cuts you up into the tiniest pieces, until you feel you don't exist at all.

Sean is like a butter knife because no matter what he says or does, he really has no point.

Sean is like a butter knife because no matter how sharp he thinks he is, he will always remain dull.

Sean is like a butter knife because, though he's only tarnished silver, he thinks he's shining gold."

As I recite, my eyes are lasered forward, focused on a tiny black mark on the back wall of the classroom so that everything else just fades into my blurred peripheral vision. I know that if I make eye contact with anyone, my voice will get stuck in my throat and I will automatically rush from the room.

I finish the poem like this, almost as if in a trance, like I've temporarily left my body and am watching the entire experience from above. It kind of makes me feel like one of those people who's gone through a near-death experience. They watch themselves die before a bright light coaxes them to heaven. Well, I've never believed in any of those stories before, not until now. But now I get it...and I feel it. I see myself going through the motions, reciting the poem aloud, but it doesn't feel like it's happening to me. I am completely devoid of all emotions, even though I am clearly revealing my entire soul to a group of strangers.

Eventually, feeling comes back to my arms and legs, and I can again sense air rushing in and out of my lungs. My vision gains focus, and I am acutely aware of the silence in the room. Every pair of eyes is glued to me and there's not a fidget or flicker in sight. No one dares look down to their phones and no one appears to be thinking about making eye contact with anyone but me.

But I am wrong in assuming they are all mesmerized by my poem and unsure how to respond. I mean, that's part of it, I'm sure, but there's clearly some deeper realization happening that I'm not fully aware of until I glance down at my hands. As if of their own volition, my hands were working away their own nervous energy while I was lost in my mind, reciting my poem. Without my realizing it, my hands have constructed a perfect origami swan, which is now resting peacefully in my palms. And when I see the swan, I feel my invisibility cloak lift weightlessly from my shoulders, as if it were a piece of silk that had been just barely veiling me all along.

They know it's me. They *all* know.

Every piece of me wants to race from the room and hide in the bathroom stall. I make secret pledges to God that I will do *anything* if He could just get me out of this situation right now. A zillion different ideas flood my brain, the impracticalities of each outweighed by my desperation. *Could I stage a false fire alarm? Could I pretend to faint? Maybe start a fight so I can get sent down to Mr. Rutter's office?*

But I don't have a chance for any of those things, because a soft and slow clapping sound emerges from the back of the room. I see Rebecca Sherman beaming from ear to ear as her applause gets louder, more demanding. Within a moment, the rest of the class joins in, some even standing and hollering their approval. I hear Mia Perkins yell, "Way to go, Jodie!" and Aiden Wilke announces to his buddies, "That was so epic!"

I am momentarily stunned, still unsure what has happened. But after a few moments, I can no longer deny that the applause is directed at me and only me. A waterfall of relief rushes over me. I scan the room and every single table of students is now standing up from their chairs, cheering and smiling. Well, except for one table. The table right at the front where Sean and Kayla are sitting.

Sean is desperately shooting daggers to anyone who glances his way, and you can imagine the fire being released from his mouth with each of his breaths. He lifts his eyebrows and throws his arms up into the air at Ms. Kelly, who has conveniently immersed herself in something on her computer screen, pretending to be detached from the scenario before her.

Kayla looks uncomfortable for once, being in the minority, and you can tell she's not sure what to do. She peers over at Sean, who is now sitting sullenly with his arms across his chest. Then, in one swift movement, it's like she makes up her mind as to which side she wants to be seen on, and she stands up too.

To his horror, Sean is left sitting by himself with the entire ninth-grade class, who are now suddenly pointing and laughing.

I know this situation all too well. I've lived it for years. Except this is the first time I'm on the other side of things. And you know what? I don't even feel bad for him.

Sean jumps to a standing position, accidentally knocking his phone and books right off his desk and to the floor. His binder pops open, the contents spilling into a heap at his feet. He bends to retrieve his phone but swears aloud when he realizes the screen has been shattered. He goes on to pick up the tiny pieces of glass, in the hope of somehow salvaging it I guess, but slices his finger in the process, causing him to curse even more. Ms. Kelly finally comes over to check if he's all right, but at this point he is so humiliated that he pushes her away, leaving a small red mark from his finger on the sleeve of her blouse. The door to the classroom slams shut with a ferocity no one expects, and the class hushes into an immediate silence. A moment later the bell rings and everyone files out as if nothing had happened. Everyone except for me. I walk out with a feeling of wonder and a sense of déjà vu. I've gone through this scenario before, only this time it's not my blood leaving a stain behind.

Chapter Twenty-One

There are those pictures, the trick pictures psychologists might show, that, when first seen, might appear to be a picture of a vase? Then the picture somehow changes and it's completely different? Like, suddenly, it's two people kissing instead, and the vase isn't visible anymore. And no matter how hard a person might try to see the vase again, there's no possibility of it. It feels like the picture has magically changed. But it's not the picture at all that has transformed. No, the picture is the same as it always was. It's simply the way it is viewed that has changed.

That's kind of what happened just now. Right after 'the new incident'. The 'coming out', shall I say?

I stagger out of the classroom, the last to emerge, and I don't really know what to do. I just sort of stand there in the middle of the hallway as students continue to bustle past, racing from class to class as if the entire world is going on like normal, as if nothing has changed. But everything has.

Out of the corner of my eye, I see a few students start to whisper back and forth. It reminds me of 'the incident', with the whispers like waves in a mountain stream, and I simply wait for the waves to make it to me.

I'm itching to run out of this building, to distance myself from what has just happened as quickly as possible. I feel as if I've been trapped in a small cage and I'm finally allowed to roam free. But before I can get away, Katie Kepperman, of all people, stands squarely in front of me with her hands on her hips and a wide grin on her face.

I'm prepared for the worst. I'm ready for the blow. *Bring it on, Katie.* There's nothing you can say about me that I haven't heard before.

But the blow I'm expecting isn't what comes my way.

"Jodie McGavin, it's you, isn't it? The origami master on YouTube? That's *you*! I have watched those videos a million times and I can totally recognize your hands. And to think that I've known you since grade school! Too cool... Remember when you came to my house in sixth grade and you taught us how to make those origami flowers? That was awesome. You're, like, famous now. And we're, like, friends and everything. So, it's kind of like I'm famous too. So cool. We could tell you had a weird, special talent, even then. Did you know that? So, are you, like, rich now? I saw you have over a million followers. That's totally epic. Maybe you could come over sometime to teach us how to make something, and we could, like, video it and put it on the feed? That would be super-cool. I would love to be doing the videos with you if you ever need someone."

"Um, yeah, thanks. I guess. Sure, that would be cool. I'll, um…let you know, okay?"

I walk farther through the hall feeling exposed, naked. But everywhere I go, people want to talk to me, to see if it's really me, to high-five and congratulate me. I was not prepared for this outpouring of support and recognition.

It's a bit too much, to tell the truth. After years of solitude, I just want things to go back to normal, to disappear into the pea-green color of the halls and melt into the dirty laminate floor, to hide in a filthy, graffitied bathroom stall until the world has stopped spinning. And I can't believe I'm actually having these thoughts.

I scramble through the hallways, dodging paper cranes and folded up frogs, in search of Bethany. I'm in desperate need of her sense of calm amid all this chaos. I finally find her waiting for Karen in the atrium, her backpack on and her cane poised in front of her.

"Hey, Beth, I'm really needing a frozen yogurt right about now. Want to come and hang out with me?"

"Jodie McGavin, it's not Wednesday, and Wednesday is the day we go for frozen yogurt. Today is Friday. Friday is pizza night. Five-thirty pizza, then a walk around the park. We need to get home before dark on Fridays."

And it makes me smile, because everything is exactly the same for Bethany, even when my existence has derailed entirely. The routines are the same, the expectations are the same, how Bethany views me is the exact same — and I love that.

I eventually convince her that we could be rebels and hit the frozen yogurt store, even on a Friday, although I have to bribe her with the promise of extra gummy bears. Those slippery, slimy candies have turned out to be her absolute favorites. I guess we've been an influence on each other, even if just a little bit.

As we walk into the store, Jared looks up at me with expectant eyes, as if he's been waiting all day to find out what happened. Bethany and I sit at our favorite booth and I wait with urgent anticipation for him to join us during his break.

"Okay, so spill the details. What happened with the poem? How did it go?"

"You won't believe how the day unfolded." I plow into a detailed description of the day's events, complete with Sean's explosive exit and the class' sudden recognition that I am the origami master they've all been following.

"So, how do you feel? Is it weird?" he asks with concern.

"I don't know yet. Maybe nothing will change and this will just be a blip on my screen of life. I'm hoping I'll just go back to school tomorrow and everything will be back to normal."

"Back to normal? Jodie, I don't think there's a possibility of that happening—at least not anytime soon. And really… Would you want that anyway? I logged onto your account this morning, and you got approved from a bunch of different advertisers. Big advertisers. Like Tiny Toys, See-Saw Games, and Gemini World Water Parks. These are massive companies, Jodie. Massive companies with *a lot* of money. You have the potential to be making thousands of dollars a month in revenue."

I honestly didn't think things would get this far. I know Jared mentioned earning money, but I didn't realize it could actually become a reality. I still don't believe it and rip my phone out of my backpack to take a look.

I log into my account and sure enough, there are display ads piled up all alongside my videos, and when I hit play for my *Learn to make a paper crane* video, a bumper ad for new basketball shoes runs for six seconds before my hands even appear on the screen.

"I can't believe this. Advertisers want to invest in me?"

"I hate to break the news, Jodie, but you really are the next big thing." Jared gives me one of his lopsided smirks as he says this, and I can't help but melt when he says the words. My fingernails are digging into my thighs underneath the table, but not out of anxiety. It's to check that this is real. That this is my reality.

I am a YouTube star.

I have taken, head-on, the biggest jerk in ninth grade.

I have a — *can I even think the words?* — boyfriend. A boyfriend who has just grabbed the hand that was pinching my thigh. Yes. This is all too real.

I click on the corner icon in my YouTube account that keeps track of my monetization so far. Already, in just over a day's worth of the ads being allowed on my channel, I've already earned almost two hundred fifty dollars!

"Seriously, Jared? I've made this much money already? In just one day?"

"I told you it could mean big bucks. The question is… What are you going to do with it and when are you going to tell your parents?"

"Jodie has big bucks! Big bucks for Jodie!" Bethany chimes in as she eats the last of her gummy bears.

"Yeah, Bethany, I guess I've got big bucks. But I'm not sure what to do with it all."

Chapter Twenty-Two

It's been two weeks since the poetry reading, since my day of 'coming out', and wow, have things gone by in a blur.

Sean went straight home that day, humiliated that for once he was the butt of other people's jokes. He returned the next day assuming everything was going to just go back to normal — but it didn't. Not at all.

For starters, and as expected, Bethany went crazy mimicking the lines of my poem over and over. *Sean is like a butter knife, Sean is like a butter knife*, and every time she said it in the hallway or in class, everyone would erupt into piles of laughter again, adding to Sean's angst. Bethany has become a bit of a celebrity in her own right and is no longer ignored in the hallway. A bunch of the kids found out how great she is at doing impersonations, and we all think it's hilarious listening to her renditions of the latest *Saturday Night Live* skit, or her replay of Mr. Stawicki's science lesson. She actually gets more attention than anyone now and kids will often try to fist-bump her in the hall—although that never really turns out great.

Second, Kayla has finally opened her eyes to see who the real Sean Fedun is—or maybe she just went along with the crowd like she typically does. All I know is that from the minute he came back to school, she snubbed him, ignoring him in the halls and sitting away from him in class. I noticed her flirting with Ty Reynolds and Chris Steadman earlier this week too, which I'm sure only helped to fuel Sean's fury. And I guess Sean just couldn't take it anymore.

His second day back to school after the poetry reading, he got into two fights because of people making fun of him, and he was sent to talk to Mr. Rutter. *Sean Fedun was sent to speak to Mr. Rutter.* That is what I call ironic. I'm not sure if even Mr. Rutter could settle things for him, though, because by the Wednesday of this week, Sean's seat in LA class remained empty and he never returned. Rumor has it that he transferred to John Franklin High, Bethany's old school, which I find even more ironic. I mean, Bethany left there because she was getting bullied, and now Sean leaves here because of the same thing. Funny how things turn out sometimes.

As for me, well I did finally tell my parents about everything that happened—the whole poetry reading, with Sean's violent outburst and everything. I was worried they would be mad, that my mom would be upset that I'd had the audacity to disrespect someone like Sean Fedun, and in public! But she just laughed. She gave out a full-force belly laugh when I showed her the poem.

"Oh, Jodie, this is just priceless! And you read it out in front of the whole class? Oh my, that must have created waves. I can't believe Ms. Kelly didn't say anything or interrupt you midway through.

"I suppose Sean Fedun must have had it coming or something. I didn't tell you this, but I went for coffee with Mrs. Sutton a few weeks ago and she was starting to have concerns about Sean and Kayla's relationship even back then. Apparently, Sean Fedun isn't the great guy everyone thinks he is. She said Kayla has come home crying a few times over recent months, complaining that Sean was being really bossy and over-controlling. She didn't get into details with me, but she did mention that she would be happy if he and Kayla ended things right then and there, that she didn't want to support their little relationship any longer because he seemed to monopolize all that poor girl's time and energy. No one should feel like that. No one. And especially at fifteen! So, it makes me glad to hear that he isn't an influence at all anymore. Perhaps he'll have a chance to start fresh at his new school."

My mom's surprising response to what I told her bolstered my confidence enough to tell her about the YouTube channel too. She couldn't believe it at first and kept re-watching the first video, just to try to make out that it is, in fact, me. So, when I told her about the money coming in, well, that was just icing on the cake. She called my dad down from upstairs and called Anna and Amy into the room so we could watch all together. We even called Granny all the way in Scotland and showed her how to log on herself with the new tablet she'd purchased, and she was absolutely smitten with the videos. She told me she was going to ask the ladies at the legion to have an Origami Night as one of the craft activities for the week, so she could show off how talented her granddaughter is. When we hung up the phone with Granny, Mom hugged me so hard that it took my breath away and told me that she was proud of me. I can't remember the last time my mom said that to me.

The next day at breakfast, Mom and Dad casually asked what I was going to do with the money. They know I'm not a huge spender, but I suppose they were worried I'd blow it on Kit Kats and Big Gulps. I told them I wasn't sure what I was going to do with the money and, at the time, that was the truth. I spent all week agonizing about how I was going to spend it in a meaningful and responsible way. Of course, I'd love to put a bunch of it aside to help pay for college. And it would be great to eventually save up for a car. But I knew I'd only be satisfied if I somehow spent some of it on something other than myself. I was kind of done focusing on *me* for a while, so I let things be for the week, continued to hang with Bethany and Jared — then it came to me. I knew how I wanted to spend the money and it made me feel good — almost the kind of good you get from finishing the last bite of a Snickers bar or making out with Jared on the park bench after school. Almost that good…but maybe not quite.

And today is the day that I finally get to put my idea into action.

The last bell of the day has just rung, but instead of rushing out to the front steps of the school to take that giant breath of fresh air I have always spent my days daydreaming about, I walk in the opposite direction, down the isolated hallway with the desecrated bathroom.

I'm not heading in there to hide in a bathroom stall. And I'm not attempting to blend into the hallway tile.

I'm holding my head high in the air as I walk into an empty classroom at the end of the hall. Well, a previously empty classroom, which now sports a giant banner across the top of the door.

Wings of Change – The Bethany Robertson Foundation for Autism Support and Inclusion

And inside, I see some of my favorite people already at work. Bethany is busy in the corner creating a new origami video to stream with three eight-graders. Karen and Rebecca are seated at a table in the middle of the classroom, designing flyers for a new social skills group we're hosting. And Mr. Rutter is sitting at a desk in the corner, presumably busy marking final exams for the end of the term.

"Hey, Jodie, how's it going?"

"It's good, Mr. Rutter. Things are going really well."

"I can't tell you how excited The Autism Foundation is that you're donating the money you raise to support them. Not only that, but starting this after-school group is really going to go a long way for advocacy and exposure. Part of the issues when dealing with anyone who has special needs is just normalizing the whole thing. Education is key."

He then walks around his desk and places a hand on my shoulder.

"And I hate to say it, but I do have a favor to ask of you." Mr. Rutter's face goes all solemn and I start to worry about what he is going to request of me.

"We have a new student who will be starting in the fall. I thought if we had someone show him around a little now, it'll make his transition to Maple Ridge much smoother."

Mr. Rutter's serious expression instantly changes as his face breaks into a childlike smile. I turn my gaze to where his eyes have wandered, over to the door of the classroom.

And who walks through the door but an awkward and scrawny teenage boy wearing a teal apron and a *Hi, I'm Jared* nametag on his shirt.

I stride over to him, my mind racing.

"What? You're registering at Maple Ridge for the fall? Why didn't you tell me?"

Jared is grinning as widely as me.

"Well, with everything that's been going on with you lately, I feel like I've been maybe missing out on the whole high-school experience. I talked to my mom the other night and she was totally in. She said it was up to me and that she'd support my decision. So here I am!"

He reaches out and grabs my hand, giving me a reassuring squeeze.

I turn and walk back to Mr. Rutter, who has been enjoying the surprise immensely.

"You know, Jodie, I'm really going to miss spending those Tuesday mornings with you every week. I always looked forward to that. But I just don't think you're going to need me meddling into your business next year. I think you've got a pretty good grip on things around here, and a pretty awesome group of friends to spend your time with."

I smile a real smile when he says this, because, in all honesty, I'm going to miss Tuesday mornings with Mr. Rutter as well.

"But, Mr. Rutter, you'll see me every Tuesday afternoon when we run the Wings of Change Club together anyway."

"Yeah, yeah, I know. It's just hard for me to believe you will be choosing to stay after school every week. I never thought I would hear those words spoken from your mouth. Remember when you thought I was a deadbeat for choosing to be a high-school counselor?" He gives me a knowing wink at this and arches his eyebrows.

"Well, I didn't actually ever say the word 'deadbeat'. I just had a hard time understanding why anyone would ever choose to spend their days here. But now I kind of get it, and it's really not so bad. Maybe there's a place for me in high school after all."

"There always was, Jodie McGavin. You just had to find your tribe."

And I did.

Want to see more like this?
Here's a taster for you to enjoy!

The Edge of Brilliance
Susan Traugh

Excerpt

Her wail reverberated off the tiled walls in a satisfying shriek. Drenched, enraged and prostrate, Amy reached her arms over her head as she lay fully clothed, sprawling half in, half out of the shower while steam roiled and the water splashed out of the open door and onto the floor.

"Manic," her dad had said. As if it was *his* word. As if he had any right to it. Any right to use it. It was hers. *Her* word. *Her* nightmare. *Her* disease.

Everyone tried to make this mess more manageable with cheery advice and condescending platitudes. But it was a curse. A plague. A full-blown disaster. She didn't deserve it and she'd wail at the wall if she wanted to.

Her therapist had once congratulated her on choosing the shower. He'd suggested cold water to cool her down and ease her manic episodes, so Amy purposely chose hot. Besides, the hot water mirrored her mood.

And yet, as the heat poured over her body, that rage seemed to seep out of her pores and flow down the drain with her tears. It was ending. She could feel the signs. But it was never raw rage into sublime peace. This trip to hell included a side trip through mortification and shame with a final destination of nothingness. And here it came again. After the volcano came the pit. Amy tried to hold on to her rage. As acidic as that fire burned, it was better than falling into the hole of despair that awaited her. For this was not the first time she'd locked herself away in fury. She just wanted it to be the last.

The rattle of the bathroom doorknob jolted Amy's thoughts as her mother successfully forced the locked door with the back of a spoon…again.

"Get out!" Amy shrieked, mustering all the anger she could pull from her waterlogged body before her mother opened the bathroom door. But she knew her mother had heard the change in her cries. They'd danced this dance so often that Amy knew her mother could anticipate each step, and the truth was, part of her was glad for her mom to come and pull her back from the volcano's pit.

"No," said her mother in a tone that allowed no response. Mom slowly closed the door behind her and surveyed the damage. She sucked in a quick breath, stopped, then slowly blew it out as if she were blowing through a straw. In her fury, Amy had slammed the shower door against the towel rack on the wall, shattering the tempered glass within the frame. The pebbles of glass hung in a weblike pattern on the door, glistening with the spray of the shower and looking like a thousand diamonds.

"He called me crazy!" Amy yelled from the shower floor, a new wave of rage enveloping her.

"I don't recall hearing him use that word," replied her mom.

"Manic, manic, manic!"

"Well, Amy, I'd say the shower door and living room furniture would attest to a manic episode…"

"But he can't *say* it!"

"What can he say, honey? What can any of us say when you're like this?"

Amy threw the soap at the shower wall. "But don't you get it? I don't *want* to be like this!"

"I understand that. But you will be until you start taking your meds regularly."

"I'm not crazy! I'm not taking meds for crazy people!"

"No one said you were crazy. Your father never used that word and never will. But you do have bipolar disorder. So your choice is to control your condition, or let the condition control you. We both know the choice you're making now. How's that working for you?"

While Amy wept, her mother stood staring at the wall. The steady pounding of the shower's water was the only other sound in the room. As she cried, Amy wondered if her mother would ever speak again.

"Who are you, Amy?" her mom asked.

Amy's words tumbled out as limp and water-laden as she was. "Your piece o' crap, screwed-up daughter. Isn't that what you want me to say?" And, despite herself, a new flood of angst escaped Amy's throat. Not rage, but shame, pain and aching need raced out from her soul and echoed around the shower floor. Once released, her sobs seemed to have no limits. *How could I do this again? Why couldn't I just control myself? Everybody else seems to be able to get a grip — why am I such a freak-girl? People are actually afraid of me! Afraid of me! If they could only see me now, sobbing in the shower, slobbering down my cheek. Only the constant stream of water washes my river of snot away. Oh God, what a hot mess I am. What a piece o' crap, hot mess.*

"No, that's definitely not what I want from you," replied Mom, as if she had heard Amy's thoughts. "I want a hopeful, dream-filled answer that will define your goals and pull your life forward. I don't know how to help you find it, but it's certainly not this way."

Amy had no other answer and simply lay crying in the shower. The water had washed away all her rage. The mania was ending and depression's grip was squeezing her throat. Amy knew her mom would help her. But she didn't know why she — or anyone — should, as that voice of shame wrapped its bony fingers around her skull, taunting her, teasing her. *You're such a screw-up. You're a burden on the family. Just disappear, asshole, and never burden your family again. Really. You know you understand why bipolar kids kill themselves. Wouldn't that peace be nice? It would just be so much easier... Life would be so much easier if...*

Deflated and empty, Amy had nothing left. She would have told her mother this fight was not done if she'd had the energy. She would have told her mom 'thank you' for coming to her rescue. But she couldn't open her mouth to say it. She couldn't say anything.

Mom reached up and turned off the water. She dropped a towel over the back of Amy's shoulders. "Come on, get up," she said as she slowly pulled her daughter to her feet. "Be careful not to touch the shower door or it might break all over you."

Wordlessly, she began to dry Amy's hair and face. Like a child, Amy sat on the toilet seat while her mom removed her shoes and socks then helped her discard her pants and shirt behind her towel-shield.

Amy walked out of the bathroom and toward her room in a zombie-like trance. As she passed, she glanced at the living room. Throw pillows were strewn all over the floor. The plaid easy chair was turned on its side and the flower arrangement sprinkled like confetti all over the rug.

"*Clean it up,*" her mother had said as the manic had begun. But Amy had only been able to destroy then. Now she could barely walk.

She stumbled into her room and fell onto her bed. Only when she had already lain down did she realize that her light was still on. Too tired to do anything about it, she simply threw her arm over her eyes and fell asleep.

Sign up for our newsletter and find out about all our romance book releases, eBook sales and promotions, sneak peeks and FREE romance books!

About the Author

Jennifer Walker is a teacher and writer from Edmonton, Alberta, Canada. She lives with her husband Ian, her two children Everett and Kennedy, and her impossibly sweet Bernedoodle puppy Leo. When she's not teaching, writing, or reading, you can most likely find her in a yoga studio, in the kitchen baking muffins, or running off the calories of the muffins she's just baked. She's famous for publicly embarrassing her family by singing terrible show-tunes and practicing 90's dance moves, and if this whole writing thing doesn't work out, she's pretty sure she could make it as the fifth Wiggle.

Jennifer loves to hear from readers. You can find her contact information, website details and author profile page at https://www.finch-books.com

Manufactured by Amazon.ca
Bolton, ON